600003152846

KT-167-850

From the Chicken House

This is an astonishing novel. Just read it.

OK, I'll tell you a *little* about it.

With a tethered earth, floating towns and rivers of sand, it's a thrilling sci-fi Western. But at its heart is true friendship in the face of peril.

And did I say brilliant? Extraordinary and like nothing else I've read? Philip Webb is a god (no, that's *not* a clue!).

Barry Cunningham
Publisher

WHERE THE ROCK SPLITS THE SKY

PHILIP WEBB

Chicken House

2 Palmer Street, Frome, Somerset BA11 1DS

Northamptonshire Libraries & Information Services NW	
Askews & Holts	

Text © Philip Webb 2014
First published in Great Britain in 2014
The Chicken House
2 Palmer Street
Frome, Somerset, BA11 1DS
United Kingdom
www.doublecluck.com

Philip Webb has asserted his right under the Copyright, Designs and Patents Act 1988, to be identified as the author of this work.

All rights reserved.
No part of this publication may be reproduced or transmitted or utilized in any form or by any means, electronic, mechanical, photocopying or otherwise, without the prior permission of the publisher.

Cover design and interior design by Steve Wells
Typeset by Dorchester Typesetting Group Ltd
Printed and bound in Great Britain by CPI Group (UK) Ltd, Croydon, CR0 4YY
The paper used in this Chicken House book is made from wood grown in sustainable forests.

1 3 5 7 9 10 8 6 4 2

British Library Cataloguing in Publication data available.

ISBN 978-1-909489-29-5

For Graham Parker

Stories come from somewhere – this one comes from USA 1991.
Five thousand miles, two travellers, one Dodge Van!

HELL'S COMING

Leaning against the doorpost of the smithy, I pretend it is a normal day. For the thousandth time in the last hour, I wonder whether I should say goodbye to Luis or just slip away. The boardwalk outside is as bright as the forge – it always is – under the light of a sun that sits on the horizon and refuses to set. Were farewells ever easier at night all those years ago, when there was proper darkness? Before the Zone. Before the Visitors came to this world and stopped it dead on its axis. I try to picture the light of the moon. Silver, so people say.

Luis pulls the last horseshoe from the furnace, lays it

on the anvil and hammers it into shape. Cisco waits patiently, ignoring the roar of flames and the clatter of new steel.

I'm not so patient. I must go. Today. But it's not like I'm going for ever. Except I most likely am. If I'm honest.

Luis pulls up his goggles and shakes the sweat from his head, watching it sizzle on the anvil. 'Is not so long since Cisco here before,' he says.

My shrug is awkward. This nonchalance game is harder than it looks.

'Maybe you like it, this place, too much.' He grins at me.

'I just don't like leaving it 'til his shoes are worn right down.'

His shrug is genuine. 'Is your dollars. These ones last good long time. Or good long journey.'

It seems to me he's taking his sweet time about this job. He batters a clip onto the front of the shoe then dunks it in cold water. I've seen him re-shoe three horses in the time he's lavishing on mine. Like he's got something on his mind too.

'Luis . . .' He looks up and my nerve fails me. 'We never agreed on a price.'

He shakes his head. 'Is on this house. Free for amigos.'

'That's good of you but . . .' I fumble out some cash.

'*De nada.*' He waves me off, almost angrily, I think.

'No, it wouldn't be right.'

He looks me in the eye. '*Mañana*, next time . . .'

I look stupid with the money in my outstretched hand. 'Yes, next time.'

'Megan,' he sighs. 'There's no *mañana*, eh? You, Cisco – you ride into the Zone. I know this.'

'That's not true,' I blurt out. One lie hot on the heels of another.

'To find your *padre*. New shoes for Cisco, supplies from Betsy's – blankets, tins, ammunition.'

I look at him aghast. I know Marfa is a small town but I thought I'd been careful with my preparations, spreading them out over several months.

'I see you gaze west always. You talk many times about the Zone, but you stop this talk weeks back. So, stands up to reason. You leave now.'

He waits for me to confirm or deny, but still I don't speak.

'But no *adios*.' He sounds hurt.

'I wanted to. I really did but I didn't want to make a fuss. I mean . . . I'm going alone. If you had any notion about tagging along then just forget it, because it's too dangerous, you know that.'

'More danger even than going solo?'

'Luis, I have to.'

'I know. And I'm coming also.'

'Now wait just a minute!'

'They find another boy for this place. I have dollars . . .'

'No, Luis. I'm going alone. You don't know the first thing about the Zone. You don't even have a horse.'

He rolls his eyes as if these obstacles are of no concern. 'I tell you, I have dollars for a horse.'

'I'm going today, just as soon as Cisco is ready, and I'm not wasting time while you bargain with a horse trader.'

3

'How come now? Why hurry, eh?'

It's a good question, and one that I barely know the answer to. 'I'm . . . just ready. That's all. It's time.'

'You know from the Zone?'

I nod, unable to explain. And I'm hardly going to tell him about the strange thoughts that have been arriving unbidden in my head recently. Suddenly the need to go into the Zone feels more urgent. I've recced the border a few times, even crossed it a short way in. And when I've been there, the urge comes from *inside me*. A powerful urge. I have no idea where my father is – I just know he's out there somewhere, alone, waiting, in peril. So each time I ride to the edge of the Zone, the temptation to keep on riding into the unknown grows stronger and stronger.

'*Zona de Diablo.*' Luis touches the crucifix around his neck and tries the new shoe for size against the base of Cisco's hoof. 'You think I watch my friend ride alone into this place?'

'It's not up for negotiation,' I mutter.

'*Conforme,*' he mutters back.

The truth is I can't decide whether his insistence is endearing or annoying. I've always considered this *my* mission, and mine alone. Having anyone else along for the ride will just cloud my thinking. The best Zone trackers operate solo or so the wisdom goes.

'You tell your aunt?' he asks without looking up.

'Not yet. Not that it's any of your—'

A gunshot cuts me short. Cisco tenses and his smoking shoe drops to the floor. It wasn't that far away – a couple

4

of blocks north towards the edge of town. Probably the saloon – though it seems rather early for drunken arguments. I peer along the boardwalk.

Luis curses in Spanish and steadies Cisco.

Another gunshot. This time closer.

'*Jesús y Maria!*'

Still, neither of us moves. It is a common hazard of the Welcome Saloon – one that doesn't concern law-abiding folks. The sheriff will settle it if any gamblers are still standing.

But then I hear footsteps running along the boardwalk and a figure emerges from the dusty light. He staggers up to me – Connor Fishwick – a regular from the Saloon. A man whose haggard face I know only because they throw him into the street when his credit is bad. For some moments he's so out of breath he cannot speak.

'Jesus, you the Bridgwater child? Megan Bridgwater? Hell's comin' for you. They's comin' and they want answers!'

'Hey, slow down! Who's coming?'

Luis steers me towards the back of the smithy. 'Go, now!'

'Wait! Who's looking for me? What do they want?'

'Does it matter a goddamn?' Connor gasps for breath. 'I ain't seen 'em before. Looked like bad-ass cowhands but they's maybe *Visitors* I reckon!'

'Visitors? Are you sure? How can you know?'

'Hell, there ain't no guarantees! They all look the same as us, don't they? But they sure was mean lookin'! Been askin' all over for Joan Bridgwater and Megan and waving round reward money. Daniel Gough acts the big man, "Go home," he says, "we don't want your dollars." And the head honcho, he shoots him down in cold blood. People start talkin' then, sayin' you're always hangin' round the smithy. They's coming, Megan.'

I wrestle free of Luis. 'Finish Cisco! Do it now!'

I figure he's going to argue but he sets to it. I peek down the boardwalk. There are two silhouettes swaggering down the street, leading their horses, guns drawn. Throughout the neighbourhood I hear the sound of shutters and slamming doors. Connor Fishwick has already fled.

'Hurry, Luis!'

He mumbles something, his mouth full of nails. More figures tramp into view. I didn't even think to bring Pa's gun today – everything is back at my aunt's shack together with my expedition pack.

Luis hammers the last nail home. I throw myself into the saddle.

'Wait!' he cries.

Trust a farrier to insist on rounding off the job when your life's at stake. But I've heard him talk through his skills enough times – if the shoe isn't seated properly it can injure the horse.

'*Completo!*' he shouts. He tosses his tools to one side, and for a moment we stare at each other.

I should go, straight away. But if I do I won't see him again. No time for goodbyes – it isn't how I've imagined this at all. My departure was meant to be a dignified, heroic affair. I steal a last look at him – wiry and tall, puffing slightly from his efforts, white burn scars on his arms and shoulders, the shape of his head under close-cropped hair, and those dark, dark eyes. Cisco paces the floor of the smithy, restless for a command.

I hold out my hand to Luis. They'll kill him if I leave him here. He grins and swings up into the saddle behind me. A shadow falls across the entrance. Luis grabs me round the waist as I spur Cisco forward.

A DAY LONG
FORESEEN

'**D**uck!'

I feel the doorframe scraping my hat but we're clear, leaping over the boardwalk rail down into the street. Three of them fall back – heavyset men brandishing rifles. Cisco misses a step but his balance is good, turning as I whip the reins around. He bucks as we tear south and west, away from the main drag towards the sharecropper fields outside town. I lie low against Cisco's mane, waiting for gunfire, but none comes. A quick glance over my shoulder and I can see they're already mounted up in pursuit. I count six, but in all the dust and sunset light I'm not certain.

'Not home!' Luis yells in my ear. 'They know your name.'

'Got to!' I shout back. I've never seen eye-to-eye with my aunt but I'm not leaving her defenceless against these men. Besides I can't think of entering the Zone without my expedition kit. It would be as good as suicide.

I weave Cisco through the streets, over fences and past trashcans, down tight alleyways, trying to shake off the hunters. *Are they really Visitors? What do they want with me?*

When the town thins out and it's just a straight sprint to my aunt's place over dry fields, I risk another look back. But I can't spot anything through the clouds of dust we've kicked up. In less than a minute, I can see my aunt ahead, beating a threadbare rug on the porch.

'Where in God's name have you been?' she snaps.

Luis jumps clear as I skid Cisco to a halt. Then I scramble to the hidey-hole under the decking. My aunt watches me drag the expedition pack clear. It's all as I left it – bedroll, provisions, water bottle, Pa's revolver, my Rand McNally map of the Zone.

'The pigs don't muck themselves out,' she says, waving her carpet-beater.

I haul the expedition pack over to Cisco and strap it on tight.

'There's no time,' I begin. 'It's not safe here any more. There are outlaws or worse coming for me. Your cousins at the Lomax ranch – go there until it's safe to come back.'

My aunt's face turns from thunder to disbelief. 'Outlaws? Where do you think you're going?'

'I'm going to find Pa.'

Other families have come to stand at the edge of the patch to witness the commotion. There's no sign yet of my pursuers.

'I'm not having you head off on your own on some fool mission into the Zone . . .'

'I'm not going alone. I'm going with him.'

She gawps for a second at Luis then marches down from the porch, gripping the carpet-beater firmly.

'The hell you are. Get back into the house right now. You're not too old for the strap, my girl. I'm not arguing with you, Megan.'

'And I'm not arguing with you, *Joan*.' Using her name emphasises the fact that she is not, and never can be, a substitute for my mother. 'I'm going right now. And if you have any sense at all, you'll move out while you've still got the chance.'

I strap on Pa's holster belt and six-shooter.

For the first time in a long time, my aunt actually stops and listens. A tiny smile creeps onto her face. 'You're fifteen, Megan. With next to no experience of the Zone. You're not a tracker . . .'

I climb into the saddle.

'I know enough. What Pa taught me.'

'You can't go.'

'I've waited too long already.'

Her hands drop to her sides then. She looks unexpectedly bereft.

'I haven't broken my back to raise you just so you can hightail it off into that godless country and get killed.'

'Megan,' murmurs Luis. 'We go now!'

But suddenly it's hard to just leave my aunt – this is an exchange that's been brewing between us for years. 'Get killed? Like Pa? Is that what you mean? Is that why you don't go after him – because you just gave up your own brother for dead?'

'Because he made me promise!' she shouts. It is very rare for my aunt to raise her voice. It takes a moment for her words to sink in.

'Because he made me promise,' she says again, this time quietly. 'There are things you don't know, Megan.'

'Promise what?'

'To keep you safe, to not follow him where he was headed. The Zone has no pity. Your mother died there right after you were born. Your father – he couldn't face losing you to the place too.'

In the silence that falls then, I realise the neighbours aren't looking at us any more. I follow their anxious glances. And from every direction I see horsemen closing in across the fields through the withered remains of crops. They ride with slow purpose, panning the land, their rifles pointing to the sky.

I look once more at my aunt. She stares back with wild eyes. And I realise this is a day she has long foreseen, hoping and praying it would never come. And now it's too late.

I back Cisco away, ready to make a charge for it.

'Wait!' she cries.

11

She scurries back to the porch and starts to root through our pitiful belongings. I stay the reins though I don't know why.

'Megan!' warns Luis.

There is no sense of urgency from the horsemen. They saunter abreast of each other, closing off all approaches with an easy menace – west, south, north . . .

My aunt returns and holds something out to me with trembling fingers. It is a folded piece of paper.

'What's this?'

'A man brought it to me. From your father. Now go.' A new resolve has entered her face.

'What man?'

From under her skirts she produces a small pistol. The way she cocks it makes me think she's always been armed this way.

'Your only chance is to go back to town. The sheriff – he'll protect you if anyone can. Go!'

'But Pa – you know he's alive?'

'I . . . was wrong to think him dead. Visitors mean to take this world, Megan. Your father – I think he's the only one who can save us now.'

A fierce hope surges in me. I have known in my heart that my father is alive – always. Only death will break the bond between us. There's sorrow in my aunt's eyes as she stares at me. I think she will say something. But then a single gunshot rings out across the scrub.

She staggers to her knees and crumples to the dust.

'NO!'

Just her blood-soaked skirts move in the wind.

12

Only then do I react. It is raw instinct – no thought for anything apart from staying alive for a few moments more. At the edge of earshot, I hear riders whoop and urge their steeds into the chase. I wheel Cisco round. He rears and jerks at the reins, desperate to be gone. Luis keels into the dirt, yelling something at me, though I can't make it out. He snatches up my aunt's pistol, meaning to stay and fight. But I cannot leave him.

I dig Cisco in the flanks, lean down from the saddle and grab hold of Luis by the collar. He catches my arm, scrambles back onto Cisco's rump and we're away. For the first few strides, I haven't got a clue where I'm headed – just alongside an irrigation ditch at the back of our patch. Anywhere will do.

'Back to town!' cries Luis. 'The sheriff!'

A LAST-STAND SITUATION

I leap the ditch, up the bank and onto the road that leads into Marfa. Cisco gets into his stride and Luis clutches onto me. For a sickening moment I think I have mislaid the folded paper, but, no, I still have it, scrunched up in the reins. I stick it in my pocket.

There is only the pumping clatter of Cisco's hooves as we charge into town. No gunfire. The streets of the centre are deserted. It's as if the place has been forewarned not to harbour us under threat of the outlaws.

We gallop unopposed into the main square, past the saddlers and the church, up to Marfa Jailhouse – a decrepit former hotel stationed close to the old courthouse.

The sheriff, it seems, is waiting for us. He jumps down from the boardwalk, eyes me briefly under the brim of his hat and strides out past us into the square, his hand hovering over his holster. I follow his gaze to four riders at the end of the street. They slow up side-by-side, trotting cautiously, peering up at roof-tops as they advance. But as they approach the square, they turn and disperse into different side streets.

The sheriff stares at the empty road, deep in thought. 'How many 'part from them four?'

'Maybe twenty,' answers Luis.

He signals for us to dismount, then lets out a sharp whistle and a skinny Mexican boy runs down the steps of the jailhouse.

'Señor Sheriff.'

'Stand down, son.' He tosses the boy a coin. 'Now listen. I want you to take this horse to the paddock by the Palace Diner. You're to stay with it 'til this thing is over. You understand?'

'Sí.'

The boy scurries away, leading Cisco by the reins. The fact that he seems to be the sheriff's only assistant worries me – where are the rest of his men?

Once we're inside the jailhouse, the sheriff locks the door and leads us through empty corridors, past steel-bar gates to a windowless cell. There is not another soul in the place. He gestures for me and Luis to sit on the swing-down bed. His face shines in the buttery glow of a single oil lamp.

'Where are your deputies, Sheriff?' I ask at last.

He does not answer, just looks at us in subdued fury. I glance at Luis, wondering if we have made a mistake coming here.

'Put your head back.'

'What?'

He puts his hand roughly on my forehead and thumbs my eyelid back so I cannot blink. Luis jumps up, but the sheriff reaches for his gun with a swiftness that takes my breath away.

'Take it easy, son. I ain't keen to see more blood spilled today.' He says it quietly, without a fuss.

He holds me like this, gazing into my eyeball 'til it starts to stream. Then he lets go and slumps back against the wall of the cell, apparently calm again. I know what he's thinking – that I could be a Visitor, one who has stolen human form to walk on the Earth. I've heard you can tell by looking at the eyes though I don't know what the signs are.

'You think we're abductee?' Luis breathes at last. 'You think *they* come here like this for help?'

'I ain't taking no chances.'

It is clear though that he suspects only me, not Luis.

'What's the sign?' I ask. 'How do you know I am not one of them?'

'Gold in the eyes,' the sheriff mutters. 'Like fire. Sometimes bright as a match flaring, sometimes just a glint.

And sometimes it slips away for a while. But it always comes back you wait long enough.'

He stares at me a while longer, deep in thought, before holstering his gun at last.

'Do you intend to lock us up?' I ask shakily.

'We're just talking. I got a manpower situation ongoing and this here's the best place for you right now.'

'What kind of manpower situation?'

'We'll get to that.'

He wipes the bottom of his moustaches and stares at me with hard blue eyes. There's a note of regret in his words, though they chill me all the same.

'Figure you're the Bridgwater girl. Your aunt said if you showed up alone, meant she was dead.'

I nod. The bare fact renders me speechless. It seems impossible. Just minutes ago she was beating a rug on our front porch. *She is dead.*

He sighs. 'I'm sorry to hear that, Ma'am.'

'How did you know I was coming? What's going on?'

'Megan, your aunt came by to see me a month back. Said she figured one day a heap of trouble was gonna make its way to the town. But she wouldn't say what.'

Why did she not say more? Didn't she trust the sheriff? He waits for me to say something.

'I . . . I don't know,' I manage at last. 'I mean, I don't think she expected trouble today, so soon.'

'But just exactly why was she expecting trouble? How come you got the meanest outlaw outfit this side of the Rio Grande riding you down?'

'You know who they are?'

'Jethro Gang,' the sheriff mutters.

My blood runs cold at the name. They are notorious outlaws, harrying the towns on the Zone border, and they kill without mercy.

I'm desperate to look at the folded-up paper from Pa. I finger the edges of it in my pocket. *Should I trust the sheriff? It is clear my aunt has told him nothing.*

He sighs. 'Megan, you are right at the eye of this here storm. I know that much. And I'm short-handed here, so I don't have the patience for nothing but the truth, you hear me?'

I figure I have no choice. The sheriff will not help unless he trusts me.

'My aunt said Visitors mean to take this world from us, reckoned my pa was the only one who could save us now. This is from him.'

With shaking fingers I unfold the paper. It is a map, scrawled in a hurry by the look of it. There are mountains and something that looks like a spider and dotted lines. One line divides the map in two and has a name scrawled on it: Mavis Pilgrim. I try to recognise landmarks but none of the mountains are named. I can make nothing of it.

The sheriff takes it from me for a better look. We all crowd around it. Perhaps the spider is a clue – if it is indeed a spider. It has eight legs, but it might be something else, like a childish drawing of the sun. There is also what looks like a cemetery – humps of ground marked with crosses.

'Mavis Pilgrim,' mutters the sheriff, tapping the name.

'Do you know her? Is she a tracker?'

'Ain't the name of no woman. She's a stagecoach. Runs mail between Zone towns – from Hope to Truth or Consequences 'cross the San Andres Mountains. But I don't know about nothing else on it.' He hands back the map. 'Figure it weren't finished. Or it's for someone who already knows them places.'

'It is meant to lead to my pa, I think. He's somewhere in the Zone, I know he is.'

He does not reply for a long while.

'Jethro Gang – they abductees, Sheriff?' asks Luis. 'They Visitors?'

'I don't know. But they seem mighty fired up to get to Megan.'

The silence in the cell is complete. For a few moments, I cannot comprehend the speed of these events and my head just swims. It is as though unearthly forces are gathering just outside the whitewashed walls, waiting to devour me. I picture my aunt lying dead at the edge of our patch. There has been little love lost between us during the years since Pa disappeared into the Zone, but she was a decent woman. I never understood why she refused to go on the trail of her missing brother. I thought she was a coward. I see now that she stayed in Marfa to see me through childhood out of a sense of duty. A promise to Pa . . . *How has this happened so quickly?* I cannot think straight.

'You figure those outlaws know about the map?' I ask at last.

'I don't know nothing except we got ourselves a heap

19

of trouble. I sent deputies out to four suspected shootings already today. And they ain't come back. I got a real bad feeling about my men being pulled every which way. If they don't show in under an hour I'd say we've got ourselves a last-stand situation.'

FOREVER DUSK

The sheriff leads us out of the cell back to the office at the front of the jailhouse. The street outside is empty and quiet. He just listens to the silence and fills his pipe, smoking in an unhurried way. His face is intent and grave. It is an uncharitable thought, but I am concerned that the sheriff is weighing his options and that one of them is to hand us over to save his own hide.

'You think your deputies are going to make it, Sheriff? Maybe we should make a break for it?'

I walk towards the front door for a better look outside, but the sheriff puts his hand up to halt me. He steps to a gun rack on the wall, and to avoid being seen through the windows, he keeps clear of the constant spokes of sunlight that have bleached the floorboards all these years.

'Figure that's what they expectin' us to do. So we're sittin' put.'

He unlocks a rifle with a mounted sight and loads up a satchel with packs of ammunition.

I throw a questioning look at Luis. And he answers it with a look of his own. This does not seem a sensible tactic to either of us.

'Sir, do you think that's a good idea? I mean, they could have us surrounded.'

'And then some.'

He edges to the frame of one of the unshuttered windows, peering into the street beyond.

'You holding anything back from me, Megan?' He says at last, without taking his eyes from the street.

'No, Sir.'

'They take pot-shots at you on the way here?'

'No, but . . .'

'Just wondering how come them riders killed your aunt in cold blood but they ain't loosed one bullet your way yet.'

This has not occurred to me. But he is right.

He sighs, to break the tension perhaps. 'I'da known yesterday what I know now, I'da taken you and your aunt out west myself, deep Zone. Tracker I know of up in White Sands. Old buzzard by the name of Devon Marshall. That's what I'da done, before them sumbitches got within forty miles of Marfa Town. And if anyone knows the lands north of the Mavis Pilgrim route it'll be old Marshall.'

'Still not so late, Sheriff,' says Luis. 'Head into wild Zone country now.'

His face creases into a weary smile. 'If we got far as Betsy's Dry Goods it'd be one of the Lord's miracles.'

He draws back away from the windows, sweeps all the files and papers off the duty desk and lays down the rifle and his two handguns.

'Know how to load these firearms if I need you to?'

We nod.

He sits in the chair and sets his boots on the desk, spurs scratching the surface. Then he motions us to sit by the doorjamb while he hands me the satchel of ammunition.

'I won't lie to you, Megan. Shoulda heard from my deputies by now. Which means they ain't coming. Just us three. Which adds up to the worst kinda trouble.'

'What's your plan?'

He smiles at that. 'Well, right now we wait for them to make a move. They ain't stormed us yet which means they working out what to do. If they wanted you just dead that'd be a cinch – just come in all guns blazin'. So, they want you alive which is just about the only ace we hold.'

He waits for me to follow the logic.

'This has to be about my pa, you reckon?'

'Yep. I'd say that was a fair summin' up. They sure wouldn't bother with some dust-bowl farm kid ordinarily speakin'. No offence.'

'None taken.'

'Obliged.' He grins at me. 'Don't get me wrong.

They're in charge of this hand. And it's their play. But we're in with a chance.' He checks his rifle barrel is true. 'Cos I sure ain't in a hurry to keep any of *them* alive. They be Visitors then they got their own Visitation Day comin'.'

Visitation Day – I was not even born yet when the world stopped turning, twenty years ago. It is hard for me to imagine that moment, though I have heard the tale many times, for I have never seen the light of the moon or a sunrise.

Pa rushed out of our old cabin in Marfa, fearing the end of days. The time by his old pocket watch was a quarter before seven and the sun was a bloated, misshapen ball of orange fire, dust-streaked and snagged at the edges by the Texas sky. And so it remains today, unmoved. Waiting for a night that will never come. But he did not know that then. He was staring towards the east at the full moon. Its destruction was not violent, he told me, when I was old enough to understand. It simply parted like someone had halved a cheese with wire. The pieces twirled away from each other, spinning in the light of the sun, breaking slowly into smaller and smaller pieces until there was nothing but a great drift of moon rocks, like a hanging cloud.

People ran out of their houses and threw themselves on the ground to pray. Dogs howled. Tides ceased. End-time preachers couldn't believe their luck. Their pronouncements were at last, after many false prophecies, coming true. But the four horsemen of the Apocalypse did not ride into Marfa, or into any other town. It was, Pa said, not God's judgment but a new reckoning. In those twenty years, the world has become a different place – from the frozen wastes of the east to the burning deserts of the west. We are still holding our breath, wondering what it means. And stranger things still have happened since.

Men and women were lost that day from a small outpost in the Sea of Tranquillity. No one knows what became of them. But most educated people agree, the moon did not come apart at the seams of its own accord. It was a sign. A warning perhaps. A visitation, though the Visitors have rarely shown themselves.

Folks say that time drags ever more slowly now that the sun holds its position in the sky. Pa used to say that the years will weigh more because people cannot just draw a line under their bad days – the unshifting angle of the sun locks them into the same black mood. But it is normal for me. Now, when I think of a world that spins, I picture a place of unsettling movement, treacherous and fleeting, where shadows are no longer nailed to their masts. Where not even the earth and rocks can be relied upon to keep their solid colours and shapes.

Time is in the whisper-ticking of my watch, in the random loops of a fly.

The day ebbs away.

I think of my aunt, and slowly lay her memory to rest.

Luis whittles at a stick with his knife.

The sheriff smokes.

'I knew your father,' he says at last, so suddenly it makes me jump. 'Before Visitation. Before the forever sunset. Strange fish, I made him out to be, them days.'

He doesn't look at me, just squints at the smouldering pipe bowl in his hands. 'Found an empty pick-up pulled over on Route 67 one winter's night. It was cold enough to freeze your spit on the way to the ground. I set my cruiser up so's I could pan the desert with headlamps. And out in the dirt was a man just standing there. I figured he'd froze in his boots, cos he never flinched when I hailed him. I got spooked when I saw the breath smoking out his mouth so I drew on him. And still he never broke off gazing at the horizon. Told me he was watching for the Marfa Ghost Lights. We got tourists and local kids in the summer spying out for flying saucers and some such. I always figured it was bull – just reflections in the air of headlamps or campfires. Just shows you how wrong you can be. Anyhow, I left him to it. No law against watching the night sky even if it's minus thirty.

'It was your daddy. I only knew him to be a teacher up in Alpine. Someone you'd tip your hat to in the street. No trouble, but not *memorable* neither.'

He tips out the ash and scrapes the pipe bowl clean. 'I sure remembered him after Visitation. One of the only clear heads in the whole county. He talked sense to whoever'd listen. Said we had to pay attention to the Zone, to *study* it. Else it'd be the end of us.'

I wait for him to continue but it's like the sheriff has exhausted his supply of words. I ask to know more, but he just busies himself with fresh tobacco. All he says further on the matter of my father is what I already know.

'First of the trackers. Figured out the craft. Listened to

the Zone so hard he lost himself in it.'

I listen to the lazy buzz of the one fly left alive in that smoky haze. I listen to the sheriff draw and puff. Draw and puff. There are fitful bouts of sleep, troubled dreams that wake me too soon.

And then the shooting begins.

THE DEMON WITHIN

Gunfire punches through the windows and the door at head-height. Straight away, Luis and I scramble under the duty desk. The sheriff follows, leaning over us as glass and plaster hail into the walls like grapeshot. The door is nothing more than splinters above the handle.

'I thought they wanted me alive,' I whisper during the lull.

'Hush!' He passes Luis a handgun and nods towards my six-shooter, still in its holster. 'You gonna draw that any time soon?'

I pull it out and it's so heavy I need two hands.

Another volley of rounds rattles the air – this time shotgun shells peppering the wall behind us.

Shouts and answering gunfire from a nearby building. *An ally?* Someone is screaming in the street beyond. I chance a peek round the side of the desk, though I can see very little through the dust. The sheriff edges past me toward the ruined door, keeping to the shadows. Another exchange outside, and footsteps pounding along the road. Then two rifle shots.

It is silent for the longest time. Luis crawls out and stations himself below a window. I feel isolated and redundant by the desk. When I cock my gun, the sheriff throws me a furious look as though I have tipped the balance of the battle with that telltale sound.

And from above the ceiling timbers comes a faint creaking. The sheriff swivels onto his back and lets rip with the pump-action. A great clod of debris spews into the room and for a moment I can see nothing but billowing grit. A stifled cry . . . Then an awful thud like a flour sack splitting on the sidewalk outside. I claw the dust from my eyes with one hand. The revolver is as heavy as a branding iron – I cannot keep it still.

'Game's up, Sheriff!' cries a voice from outside. 'Yer deputy's hit in the belly. The cavalry ain't coming any time soon. Send out the girl and we'll make it quick for you, I give my word.'

The sheriff gazes back at me with a tiny shake of the head. 'She's down too,' he yells back. 'Can't move her.'

'Yer a lyin' dog. Can't hear nothing from her.'

I take a deep breath to start groaning, but the sheriff

warns me off the act with a wag of his finger. 'Sounds a might like Bud Haslett,' he cries. 'Except it ain't. He disappeared last year out huntin' buck Terlingua way and he ain't been seen since.'

No answer.

'Bud was a Christian soul what never held company with outlaws. Well, listen, whatever-the-hell-you-are, the girl in here took one in the gut. I'm tellin' you, she'll be needing a priest if you don't rustle up a saw-bones from some place next five minutes. Leakin' like a stuck pig in here.'

There's a pause. Perhaps they've fallen for it, though I cannot see how it helps us. Except, if they're desperate for me to remain alive, then they will not delay . . . My reactions are sluggish as though emerging from hibernation. As footsteps charge up the sidewalk steps, the barrel of my gun lolls to and fro, mostly at the floorboards.

But the sheriff is already on his feet, standing square in the sunlight with his shotgun held out low by his hip. He waits, he waits. And . . . BOOM! Wood panels spiral away from the entrance. He pumps another shell into the chamber. A flurry of movement at the smashed doorframe. BOOM! He strides forward, taking it to them now. A figure blasts through the window and crashes onto Luis – a shadow spitting flame. The sheriff swings to face him, primes, fires. And the gunfire falls silent.

'Luis!' I cry out, standing up in full view. *Knocked unconscious? Or dead?*

Nobody moves. It is as though time has all along been a perfect shuffle of cards, riffling and slotting and sliding next to each other, but now the pack sprays out of control onto the floor.

The intruder staggers and crashes backwards.

The sheriff turns to me, his eyelids flickering. He sags to his knees. The shotgun slips from his fingers.

Long, deliberate strides bring a tall man to the threshold of the building. *Can this really be a Visitor?* He pauses to survey the scene, his shoulders blocking the light, his gun trailing by his side. I can see nothing of his face – it is locked in shadow. But his eyes flare briefly – gold, like embers in a gust of air.

He steps without concern into the office.

And, without even looking at the sheriff, he shoots him at close range. The sheriff spins with the force of the round and clatters to the floor.

No more cowering. I raise the gun. My wilting limbs seem to prop each other up. Just.

What do they want with me? My insides just let go and I soak my pants. The urine runs cold before it reaches my knees.

The intruder stops just in front of me, stuffing his belly onto the barrel of my gun. There's a grin on his face. Several days' growth. A smattering of boils across the flattened bridge of his nose. As I gape at him, the gold of his eyes spreads, in one beat, swallowing whites and pupils. And they *burn*. The flickering glow puckers the flesh and the lashes. He, *it*, is so close I hear the swill of saliva in its mouth as it licks its lips . . . Beneath the skin, I imagine a creature. Harnessed and hunched into a cloak of human flesh. Something made of molten hatred.

'Let's see if you can hit the target, cupcake,' it mocks. The voice gurgles softly, like the lungs are full of mud.

'You got the shakes? Ain't so easy to shoot a critter point blank now, is it?' The way it *talks* – summoning the speech of Bud Haslett, a man long dead – chills me to the core.

It lets its firearm drop to the floor and thrusts its gut further forward. I try to breathe, take a hold of my fleeing thoughts – this is all so *wrong* . . . *Shoot! Shoot!* But I can't. And it *knows* I can't. Its eyes blaze. And when it speaks again, there is no trace of Bud Haslett at all.

'So, it *is* true, about you.'

'W-what? What's true?'

'You don't know?'

Its leer widens. It reaches beyond the limits of what should be possible – a molar-baring snarl. Like a demon drawing back the cheeks from within.

I stumble away.

Its skin is hitched so high from the teeth that I think it will tear, and at last the grin slackens with a jowly pop.

A hot sour stench envelops me as its voice bubbles up, loose with phlegm.

'Come to me,' it whispers. 'Let me show you the answers you seek, about what will become of you and humankind. Bridgwater child.'

I *must* shoot. But unnatural visions are flashing through my mind. *People all in a row, waiting, until light swallows them and they scream without sound, their mouths hinged back, jaws breaking right open, their faces unfurling like dreadful flowers . . .*

I sway backwards, dropping the gun, and stagger into the corridor that leads back to the cell. I fumble at the barred door and swing it shut with all my weight. The latch snaps fast.

The intruder follows me, leans its head against the bars and closes its eyes with a dead smile. The eyelids just wrinkle black and drop away smoking, as the orbs beneath them shine out. It grips the bars so hard the fingertips split open and by degrees the steel begins to yield.

But then, as convulsions take hold of its shoulders, I see the sheriff stir from the floor behind. A single shot rings out and wet heat slaps into my face.

ZONE QUIVERS

Even as the Visitor slides down the bars, the life goes from its eyes. A piece of its head the size of my fist is missing. Something like a fat worm wriggles from the skull and flops dead against the side of its face. My mouth is salty from blood – the stolen blood of Bud Haslett.

My breathing is chaotic. In a small voice I call out, but neither Luis nor the sheriff stirs. Smoke curls from the barrels of fallen guns. Strangely, I can smell it from here. I try the door but it will not budge, jammed somehow now that the bars are bent. All is quiet – no more outlaws perhaps to storm the building? If I could reach the dead

Visitor's revolver, I could maybe shoot the latch out, but it's too far away even at full stretch.

I must keep moving, keep thinking. Or my sanity will leak away. Once again, in my mind's eye I see the terrible vision – row upon row of people awaiting the plunder of their bodies. I turn, meaning to find a different way out, and hear the crackling for the first time. Firelight jumps from the corridor and, within moments, snatches the ceiling beams. A river of smoke rolls towards me.

'LUIS! SHERIFF!'

The yelling makes me cough and I sink lower to avoid the fumes. I rattle at the door uselessly, then jam my arm up to the pit to try again for the butt of the Visitor's gun. Even at full stretch my straining fingers are a good metre short.

But the Visitor is within reach. Maybe it has another weapon. I pad frantically at the jacket and the pockets above its chaps. Chain watch, key fob, tobacco pouch. The possessions of an abductee – kept as what? Trophies? Cover? I hold my breath 'til my chest burns and then I hold it some more. My eyes stream. I feel the heat at my back. Sparks settle on my skin. The crackle of flaming timber becomes a roar. I claw at the dead man's clothes 'til my hands are slippery with blood.

Someone screams my name.

I can see nothing. Just a smudged hump moving through the gloom. I gasp for breath and take down only noxious fumes. My lungs pinch shut.

A single gunshot and the scraping of the door. A hand at my collar, dragging me clear.

'Megan!'

Luis!

We scramble away from burning walls, tumbling out into the sweet cold air. I choke and retch, and I can't see, my eyes are so raw.

The sheriff has been dragged clear too. The Mexican boy tends to him by the kerbside. But as I draw closer, it's clear that he is in a bad way. His shirt is steeped in blood and his skin is grey.

'We go now,' urges Luis. 'Is nothing to do for this man.'

'Wait.'

I cradle the sheriff's head. I don't think he can see me, the way his eyes wander, but he smiles and tries to say something. I drop my ear to his mouth but it's gibberish.

'No time,' groans Luis.

'He saved my life. I'm not leaving him here.'

The sheriff finds the strength to raise his voice. 'Get gone, Megan. I ain't riding nowhere.'

'You need a doctor.'

'Be here soon enough. There'd be nothing to patch up if that last one could shoot straight. Never even looked. Angel on my shoulder today. Gotta shoot them between the eyes, Megan. Only way to take them down.'

'Don't talk any more.'

'Figure they ain't gone far. We just beat 'em back some. Head up to White Sands. Devon Marshall.'

His breathing runs shallow.

The jailhouse is an inferno. Flames whip in the wind, hugging the wreckage as it crumbles. The vision visited upon me is a searing mark in my brain. The silent scream of men, women and children waiting in line.

I must have a haunted look, since Luis speaks gently for all the urgency he must feel. 'Megan, we go now.'

The young Mexican boy looks up at me with tears in his eyes. 'Ride, Señorita. I find help for our sheriff. Take horses. Go!'

I kiss the sheriff's cheek and murmur my thanks into his ear. There is nothing in his expression to suggest that he understands me. It feels wrong to abandon him this way, but only a surgeon can save him now.

I check I still have the map and nod to Luis. He tosses me my six-gun and the satchel of ammunition. Across his back he has slung a shotgun and the sheriff's long-range rifle. He leads the way to two horses looped to a rail across the road – one of them, Cisco, is yanking and whinnying to get free. Luis unties a fine Appaloosa and mounts up.

'Whose is that?'

He shrugs. 'Outlaws. Mine now.'

He looks nervously down the smoke-filled street, at the bodies lying there. 'The others, they come back soon. Vamoose, let's go!'

One last look at the sheriff and his young charge, then I jump into Cisco's saddle and dig my heels into his flanks.

'Where to?' cries Luis.

'Davis Mountains,' I yell over my shoulder.

I am vexed about taking an outlaw's horse. It is bound to be someone's stolen property and there are towns on-Zone that carry the death penalty for rustling. Still, I cannot worry about that now. I try to blank my mind as we tear out of Marfa off the road and into open country.

We gallop west and north, out towards the desert flats and Marfa Airport.

We slow only for the abandoned trenches and barbed wire defences of the old Deadline border. To our right lies the concrete apron of the airstrip – rusted remnants of old planes tipped by the wind. I snatch glances over my shoulder but no one has given chase.

At last we enter the Zone, and there is that telltale shift, that sense in the air that the rules have changed. I feel no immediate danger ahead but we slow to a trot anyway. We may have outlaws on our trail but they are not the worst dangers here. This is a forsaken land, and from the wastes of Alaska, down through the Rocky Mountains and as far south as Tijuana, the true threat belongs to the weaknesses of the human mind.

A raw wind scrapes over the desert. I climb down from Cisco to settle him – he is jumpy after the ride from Marfa and I, too, need to calm down. Luis keeps looking back and I know he's eager to push on to the Davis Mountains where there will be cover at least. But Pa always said the Zone claims most victims when they panic, punishing their rash decisions. We must be cautious.

We continue in silence, north towards Fort Davis, staying two miles or so west of Highway 17. It makes sense to keep away from the road in case outlaws lurk there, and I steer a course along a dry gulley into the low sun to hide us from view as much as possible.

After a few miles, though, the gulley starts to lead us too far west, so I skip Cisco out of it. And that's when I get my first real inklings of worry.

Luis calls to me, 'I know. I feel it.'

Seasoned trackers like Pa call it the *quivers*, a sense that things are contrary to nature. I know Cisco feels it, too, from his sideways stamp and his necking at the reins. A change in the air. Like a tightening. Like every decision you make matters – where you put your feet, how often you breathe, how much shadow you cast. The only thing you can do is stay hair-trigger alert. Trackers get tuned in, if they live long enough. They can read the terrain and how it is changing. But me, I'm just learning, and I haven't clocked up enough Zone hours to read my quivers properly. I just know we're under threat, but what from is anyone's guess.

We thread a way through thorny breaks. Wind picking up now. The branches of stunted trees all point west to the sunset glow, hungry for light, like praying beggars. There's a scrabbling sound as they move to the gusts and squalls. Feels like a storm is on the way.

We both pull our collars up and tip our hats into the wind. I peer under my brim at the gathering columns of dust and try to plot a course towards Blue Mountain. It's a good place to enter the Davis Mountains and lies a little to the west of Fort Davis, allowing us to steer clear of roads and buildings. But it is not long before I spot the raised banks of Highway 17, dark against the amber blaze of the sun. Somehow we have strayed too far east. Grit races across the untended tarmac. In places, the road has become submerged beneath shallow dunes. Wind whistles through broken fittings high on lamp posts. A tumbleweed bounces over the lanes. Both directions are empty, though I cannot see far up the northbound stretches – a gloom has built up over the road, a bruise in the sky and across the land that could be a dust storm, though it does not seem to move. Which worries me.

'Let's cross the highway and skirt around it.'

'We go back west, no? Straight to Davis Montanas.'

'I tried that already. The Zone is pushing us here.'

'I think is danger . . .'

Rookie outbursts like this don't help one bit, but this is no place for an argument – I need to concentrate.

'Just let me do the tracking,' I say calmly. 'I'm not going to ride into it – I just want to keep it in range 'til I get more of a sense of it.'

He huffs in frustration but doesn't argue. I may not have much Zone experience but I have more than Luis.

I estimate that, whatever it is, the gloomy patch is half a mile wide, maybe more, though it is hard to tell because it is not obvious how far away it is. It has a fuzzy edge and sometimes a tendril of shade will whip out like a dust devil from the central core of a twister. But twisters have sharp outlines and are much narrower, with blasts of debris at the base. This thing just hangs there like a smudge, right over Highway 17. We avert our eyes – it is clearly something that belongs to the Zone and even paying such events too much attention can be perilous.

The dark patch is directly on our left when I hear the first baying of wolves. Cisco nearly bucks away from me in panic. I guess the wind is too changeable for him to have picked up their scent, so it is a shock they are so close.

Luis has a much harder job keeping his horse in check – it spins and rears and dances about.

I draw and cock the Colt, then scan our tracks. Four shapes are stalking the margins of the highway. They pad confidently, not bothering to keep low, and, God, they are big! The lead one pauses, a huge male, watching me as the wind ruffles the fur across his back, and twitching his ears. He throws his head back and howls. It is chilling to be so close to that eerie moan, a call of hunger that rises into the wind. Even as the howl dies, others answer it – to the front and behind us. They have us encircled.

'I not hold him!' cries Luis. 'Ride! Any place! Now!'

'Wait! Panic and we're done for.'

'Is not me! The horse panic!' His horse nearly topples as it rears with Luis practically standing in the stirrups.

'Steady him!' I shout. If he bolts, he's dead, I know it. We've only been in the Zone an hour – I should have left him behind.

We will not outride a whole pack. I must think! For the first time since the wolves closed in, I look at the strange hanging gloom. Sunlight seems to bend around it – a vast column of blurred grey peaking below real and racing clouds. The decision is made even before I fully agree to it in my mind. Both Cisco and I act, as one – kicking into a full gallop. Over my shoulder, Luis takes up the charge too – his horse desperate to follow.

Ahead, I can see nothing but scratches of movement in the mass of grey – it is like a hole in my vision, like peering through layers and layers of shifting muslin. But it is preferable to a pack of wolves on the hunt. I snatch another glance over my shoulder. Behind Luis, the beasts meet – two pincers, maybe twenty of them. There is a pause when I think they have given up the chase, but they funnel after us, undeterred by whatever it is we're heading for.

I ride 'til my eyes can see nothing but the grey gloom. I expect a refusal from Cisco as we enter something like fog, though it is dry and made up of agitated scribbles of movement. A fur of static runs over my skin and there is a burnt smell, like cordite – crackles of charge like thousands of tiny lightless sparks.

Then, we're in the clear.

It's like we've popped a giant bubble.

The grey fuzz has all just disappeared.

Cisco slides to a halt in shock, as Luis tears past me.

And there in front of us is a town. A town that should not be there because there are no towns on Highway 17 between here and Fort Davis.

But that's not the half of it. Because the entire town is hovering perhaps twenty metres in the air.

There is no time to take in this impossibility. I swing round in the saddle to see the wolves careering towards me, pitching into a new pincer movement. I fire off a round in their general direction, but they do not baulk.

I put the reins in my teeth again and re-cock the pistol with both thumbs.

The town is our only option, though I cannot see how to enter it. I spur Cisco on 'til Luis is abreast of me. The place looms above us. It cannot be real! But this is the Zone. Weird space-time wrinkles are the reality here and now. The foundations and tree roots and sewage pipes hang from its underbelly like the frills and tentacles of a vast jellyfish. It has no means of support, though the air under it wobbles, as warped as the imperfections in blown glass.

We both rein in our horses at the town's edge, not wanting to charge into the hanging jungle of cables and pipes. There has to be a way in, a way to safety.

To my right a wolf bounds towards me, trying to clip Cisco's hooves. He's so close I can see the yellow of his eyes, the snap of his jaws. I take a pot shot with the Colt and there's a whimper as he falls back. Other wolves are closing in. I can't steady Cisco to take aim.

But then another shot rings out and the dirt beside me kicks up.

There, leaning over a wall at the edge of the town directly above is a figure. Long blonde hair spills over her face as she cups her mouth and yells.

'The far side! There's a hill! It's the only way up!'

VALENTINE
REFOUNDED

The wolves are nearly upon us. We have to risk the passage beneath the town. The floating town. What if it should fall now? Clods of earth rain down as if the buildings have just been uprooted. From above comes the muted wail of sirens. No, not sirens – vehicle alarms. Which also cannot be true. In the Zone, no machines function. It must be something else. I lead the way, weaving between misshapen stalactites of concrete. A dark shaggy roof blocks off the sky. The horizon ahead is held in a vice between two grips of land, but as the blonde girl promised, there are the slopes of a hill.

The barking of the pack reaches a frenzy as I urge more from Cisco. He's tiring now, but he thunders up the hillside, where wolves bound among the shrubs. Up, up, up . . . I snatch a glance behind – Luis is just a stride away, his horse flailing in the dust.

'Come on!' I yell.

There are fissures and boulders – the route I pick is pure instinct. No second chances. If we dead-end now, the wolves will have their kill.

I hit the top, and the town opens out before me. Unbelievably, there is a police patrol car parked on the edge of a sheared-off road. Its hazards are on – blue beacons in the glare of the sun. But as I pull ever closer, I see the hitch.

There's a gap between us and the road.

Steel rods poke from the chewed-up hardcore.

Wolves are streaming up from the shadows under the town.

There's a ramp of rock at the narrowest point of the gap. But it's still a big ask. Even a fresh Cisco without all my expedition gear would be hard-pressed. *Last push*. Luis comes up beside me . . .

We both take the jump at the same moment, full stride. The Appaloosa forges ahead – lands it strong and clean. I know Cisco's given it everything. But he's too ragged . . . there's a terrible lurch as his forelegs thump into the road, belly scraping the crumbled edge, hind legs bunching in to find a hold. We stagger to a stop. Poor horse – his legs tremble and buckle. But we've made it!

Behind us the wolves gather, their jaws drooping. They dart about, looking for a way to reach us, but the gap is too great.

'Hellzapoppin', girlfriend. That was one mighty close call.' The Texas drawl is deadpan, almost bored. She gazes at Luis as he slides from the saddle, doubled up from exhaustion. 'Figured you two for wolf dinner, or breakfast. Hey, you got any idea what time it is? Hell, I don't even know what day it is. That sun sure is pretty but it ain't budged in all the time I been here. Like to say that was the weirdest thing about waking up today. But, well, you know about the flying town of Valentine, I guess.'

I hang over Cisco's mane, trying to catch my breath, staring at the blonde girl. She slouches on the patrol car hood, with her boots propped up on the fender, rifle cradled across her lap. She stares at me through mirrored sunglasses, and chews extravagantly at some gum. She is my age, dressed in an enormous shaggy fake-fur coat, industrial orange pants and red pixie boots. Pre-Visitation clothes.

Slowly, what she's just said sinks in.

Valentine? Valentine used to be on the I-90 a good twenty-five miles west of here, but every last brick of it disappeared on Visitation Day twenty years ago, together with every living soul that called the place home. There's just a crater where it once stood. And now it has returned. And the girl before me knows nothing about how the world stopped spinning. For her, all this has only just happened. She's one of the disappeared. She's an abductee.

46

'What *are* you wearing, missy? Looks like you took a wrong turn into the 1800s. What's the deal? Is it Fourth of July today? Mardi Gras parade?'

I glance at Luis as the realisation dawns across his face. He reaches for his shotgun slowly, but I warn him off with a tiny shake of the head.

'It is how we all dress now,' I manage at last. 'In the vicinity of the Zone at least.'

She slides off the hood, hefts up the rifle and pumps a careless shot at the wolves.

'*Vinner-city*? Where's that? Are we even in Texas?' Her drawl is so stretched she sounds under the influence.

'This is still Texas,' I say carefully. I feel no threat from her, but she could be a Visitor in a stolen body, like the outlaws. Equally she could have survived abduction, she might be human – why else would she help us escape the wolves?

'Are there others here?' I ask.

'Nope. SCRAM!' she yells at the wolves and aims again.

I swing down from Cisco and grab the barrel.

'Hey!'

'Enough shooting. There are people out here in the Zone worse than those wolves and I do not want to draw them here.'

'Well, listen up, Calamity Jane. I just saved your sweet ass back there, so how about you loosen up some and tell me what's going on, since you're the expert and all?'

Is this a trick? Have we been forced into a trap so soon? We must determine if this girl is real or Visitor. My quivers are silent on the matter. But I really don't like the way her eyes are hidden from view. I stare at two images of myself in her sunglasses – I look like a desperate fugitive. Desperate and scared.

'We need water for the horses,' I tell her. 'Is there any to be had in the town?'

'Sure,' she answers at last. 'Pipes are dry, but there's a water tower yonder by Denny's.'

She sounds genuine enough, but I remember the way the outlaw Visitor mimicked the voice of Bud Haslett.

'You drove that vehicle?' I point at the patrol car.

'I ain't legal 'til next summer, but my brother, Lloyd, learned me the basics . . .' She trails off, suddenly angry at justifying herself. 'What are you, the sheriff?'

I look in through the driver's window. 'Radio?'

'Dead as a drill bit, honey. Look, there's just me, OK?'

She pulls off her sunglasses. She's got mascara on, smudged like she's been crying. The tough girl act is looking frayed at the edges.

I take a pace closer and try to see if there's anything peculiar about her eyes.

'Megan,' warns Luis.

'It's OK.'

'Hey, what is it with you two? I helped you out. Now I ain't looking for a cheerleader dance, but seems like you ain't a whole lot surprised about my home town being mid-air, so maybe you can return the favour and tell me what in hell is going on?'

Another step closer. I peer hard at her eyes. They are hazel, clear whites – quite beautiful. Not a hint of golden fire. She is bewildered and scared and human, I decide. And suddenly, I feel sorry for her. There are no easy explanations when it comes to the Zone and Visitation Day. Especially for true abductees. They are notoriously fragile.

'Your town . . . disappeared,' I begin. 'It has now returned.'

'Disappeared?' She throws a suspicious look at Luis, perhaps wondering why he keeps his distance, not saying a word to her. 'Well, where's it been at?'

'I don't know.' Arguably the truth.

I look past her for Denny's. The main street ahead is torn in places and it undulates gently, which is making me feel queasy. I have heard of abductees returning in one piece, but never whole towns. Perhaps this girl is genuine, but Visitors may still lurk here, hidden for now. I fetch Cisco – he is weary but does not seem spooked by the girl's presence.

'I heard car alarms,' I say.

'Yep, they been going off now and again. I yanked out the batteries trying to give my ears a rest . . .' She skips ahead of me, like she wants to lead the way.

'Megan . . .' Luis's hand hovers near the shotgun.

'Relax, Luis.'

'Yeah, you said it. Relax, buddy. Things is spooky enough without you hitting the panic button.'

Luis fires spit at the road and follows at a distance, leading his horse. He does not take his eyes off the girl. I know what he's thinking. Even if she's not a Visitor, what can we do to help her? In towns like Marfa, they don't take chances. Abductees that return are sometimes hanged anyway. Who knows what devilry has been planted inside them?

I stare at the billboard sign for the 'Eightball Motel' – the M and the T flash and flicker. Other lights blink towards the far end of the town.

'Freaky, huh?' says the girl. I can tell she is uneasy about the silence, about Luis staying back. 'I mean, we ain't exactly hooked up to the grid no more, right? I tried TV but there ain't no signal. Look, do you know anything here? I mean, are they sending anyone, like the army or somebody?' Her voice cracks a little.

I look at her. Where do I even start?

Luis calls out to me in Spanish, 'We should not be here, Megan. The Zone drove us here, no? We can't help her.'

He is right. There is nothing we can do. But, still, it feels wrong to withhold the truth from her.

'It is not safe here for you,' I begin. 'Men will come to strip the town and they will not take kindly to abduct . . . They will not take kindly to strangers.'

'I ain't a stranger. I was born and raised in Valentine . . .'

'You must believe me. You are a stranger now. The world . . . has changed.'

She stands in front of me. 'Now, you be straight with me! What's going on? Where the hell is everyone?'

Luis reaches for the shotgun. I hold up my hand to stop him. I do not have time to explain this in any detail that will make sense to her. Her best chance of survival is to get a federal handler, someone who can examine her properly, quarantine, rehabilitation. Abductees need counsellors and I am not qualified . . .

'Please!'

'You will not be ready for the truth.'

She raises her eyes to the sky and seems to fight back more tears. 'Hell, you think you're doing me favours by keeping me in the dark here? I can see the whole town's floating off to hell in a hand basket!'

I take a deep breath and try to think how I would be in her situation. It is surely her right to know at least.

'There has been extraterrestrial contact on Earth for some time. Your town was disappeared. You and all the inhabitants of Valentine were abducted. You don't remember – no abductee ever does. You will not be able to account for the last twenty years . . .'

I swallow my words when I see the awful shock on her face, the way her eyes dart about like a cornered animal's. Her shoulders slump.

'Twenty years? But I've just been asleep for a day.' Her voice is flat and dazed.

'You won't have aged. But I can assure you that many things are different. Nineteen states are now in the Zone – a lawless area that covers the Midwest and the Pacific coast. The world has stopped spinning. The moon is now rubble.'

She gapes at me and I have no idea if my words are sinking in.

'But my family?'

'If they were here on Visitation Day then they're abductees, too.'

'Well, where the hell are they?'

'I cannot say. They are . . . missing. Some, like you, return. Unharmed. But . . .'

'But what?'

'Look, no one knows what happens to abductees. Maybe nothing. But folks here, especially around the Zone, they don't trust the ones who come back. You'd be advised to lie low, contact the authorities in Houston.' These words sound ridiculous even as I utter them. How will she even get from here back to the Deadline border in one piece, let alone Houston? 'At least there you'll be given a fair hearing.'

'A hearing? What is this – I'm breaking the law now? For not knowing what the hell you're talking about?' She gives me a tentative smile. 'You're messing with me, right? I mean . . .'

'Do you think I would joke about this situation?'

I wait for a tirade of swearing and crying. I cannot begin to imagine what questions are building inside her. But she just sniffs and looks at the endless sunset.

'Well, I guess I don't have to worry about wasting my life in Taco-Shack-O no more. Wish I'd told Wade where he could stick that job. Don't suppose he's yelling at folks to bus tables now.'

Time to concentrate on practicalities.

'I can direct you over the Deadline border. You should avoid Marfa – I'd head for Fort Stockton . . .'

'The Deadline border?'

'Zone boundary – machines start working properly east of Highway 67. It'll probably be more familiar to you – the towns and cities.'

'I'm staying. The others might show – Lloyd, Mom, Dad . . .'

I take her hand then. 'What is your name?'

'Kelly. Kelly Tillman.'

'I cannot force you to listen to sound advice, Kelly, but if you do not leave this place, you will surely die. The Zone is a graveyard for those who haven't learned its ways.'

'I've got to find them.'

I know that feeling – everyone I care about is gone too, except Luis. I stare at her eyes, glittered with tears, and know in my heart she is one of us. But she is a lost cause – I cannot afford to help her.

'What's your name?' There's a challenge in her voice, something new about her.

I turn away but she snatches at my sleeve. 'Hey, don't you turn your back! Don't you dare!'

I face her and harden my resolve. It is harsh but there is nothing I can do for her. 'I am Megan Bridgwater. I am sorry about you and your family. I have offered to direct you off-Zone but I have a heap of problems myself and I will not waste time here on your account. Take your hand off me.'

But then Luis pulls the shotgun from the belt on his back and levels it at Kelly.

DEATH-WISH SMILE

Kelly looks at him and laughs. 'Hold up, Jose. You gonna say something to me before you pull that trigger. Man, I've just about had it with you two!'

'*Silencio!*'

'Luis, it's OK,' I cry. 'Put the gun down!'

'She's liar,' he breathes. 'She wait for us to come, no? She say she wake up here. Why she not try to leave this town?'

'Well, that'd be the dumbest move ever seeing as the country's crawlin' with wolves. I been searching the whole town for signs of life – ain't that what you'd do if it was the last place you seen your folks?'

'What you know about my people?' he says.

'Luis, please put the gun away,' I plead.

'No, Megan.' He does not look at me. His face is cold. I step between them.

'Stay back, Megan. They lie, they get close, they take you. You know.'

He pulls the shotgun to one side of my boots and blasts a round into the road. The noise echoes out onto the plain.

'Move, Megan. I swear . . .'

'Would she help us if she was one of them?' I ask, trying to keep my voice even.

'Don't matter. If she don't know. Don't matter. Is what they do – hide inside.' He taps his head. 'Play innocent. Like real people.'

'Hey, I'm still here you know! Maybe you two could cut the crap and tell me straight up, yeah?'

Luis spits to one side and cranks another round into the chamber.

'He thinks you're a . . .Visitor,' I manage at last.

'What? An alien. You think I'm from outer space.' She snorts in disbelief. 'I'm Kelly Tillman, you dumb-ass. From 41 Montana Avenue, Valentine, Texas. What's left of it. I canned seventh grade for a piece-of-crap job with lousy tips and lousy hours. You ain't telling me I'm the outsider here. No way.'

'They take human bodies as their own,' I answer. 'They must if they are to walk on this Earth. Beneath the skin they are not of this world. Some abductees are returned –

truly themselves. But they are broken inside. And they are . . . not trusted.'

Luis raises his gun slowly.

Kelly narrows her eyes at me. 'So how can you tell who's regular and who's alien?'

'Their eyes are different, sometimes.' I think about the one and only Visitor I have ever seen. 'But they can mask the signs.'

'Not when they die,' adds Luis.

'Oh great. That's just cherry pie, that is. So I can't prove who I am 'til I'm pegged out on a slab. Well, hoop-de-doo, how about you're an alien, also? And Pancho over there? And Miss America? And Daffy Duck? You got proof of your membership to the human race, eh?'

'You're abductee,' says Luis.

'She's safe, Luis. I know it. Lower your gun. I trust her.'

'And him?' She glances over my shoulder.

'Fools trust,' answers Luis. 'My family, all killed by Visitors – I see with these eyes.'

Kelly steps to one side of me, and there is a clear line of fire.

'So come on then, big shot. Do the deed. You ain't gonna be sure 'til you pull the trigger so let's get it over with.'

We stand in a triangle, stuck almost, and in that moment my head is filled with a heavy pain, like an instant migraine. Not a vision this time but dozens of thoughts arriving at once, from nowhere. *Three eggs in a kestrel nest I found once. The tripod stand of Pa's camping stove. My aunt reading Genesis: Chapter 3 – the fall of mankind . . . Three, three, three . . .*

A warning from the Zone? A message from somewhere? A trick perhaps? I cannot decipher it. And then all at once the thoughts and the pain vanish.

I reach out to Kelly but she brushes me off. Luis raises the gun, but his shoulders are trembling.

'Hey, Luis. Changed your mind now? How about it? You was ready to let me have it just then. But what if you're wrong? Hmm. What do you know – she was plain old Kelly Tillman all along. Buzzard food now.'

'Kelly, don't!'

'It's OK, Megan. Just trying to clear it all up so we can move on.'

She strides up to him, so the shotgun is practically touching her chest. It reminds me of my stand-off in the jailhouse. When I was the one holding the gun.

Luis backs up. His face darkens. He chews his lip. He's angry now, to be made a fool of. He pulls up the gun.

And I think Kelly will start to crow at him, to let off her steam. But she doesn't. She just stands there.

'Are we done?' she says quietly.

He nods.

She turns to me. 'Had to be cleared up. Else it's always just hanging at the back of everyone's mind. So, we all buddies now?'

Her face is flushed deepest pink, eyes wide and bright and troubled. She turns on her heel to Luis again.

'Course if I turn out to be extra-T, then be my guest. I mean it.' Her tone is sincere.

'Same for me,' mutters Luis. 'If my body taken.'

I stand there in a daze. The two of them were spitting enemies just moments ago. Now they are sealed in a death pact against Visitors. Grim allies.

They stare for a few moments at each other, before at last Kelly grins. 'Hey, Luis, nanoo-nanoo. Just kidding. I'm kidding . . . Well, I'm all for sacking off this place just as soon as you like, but there's three of us and just two beat horses. And them wolves still sniffing about . . .'

But at this precise moment, two things happen. The lights from the Eightball Motel explode. And the road we're standing on cracks in half with a mighty noise of splitting concrete.

I brace myself for a terrible fall as a rupture runs towards us, snaking down the cats' eyes, sending up puffs of debris. A ripple crest of tarmac rides under our feet and sends the three of us sprawling. Out of the corner of my eye, the Eightball Motel tips away into nothing.

Now the town stops sliding but, as Kelly straightens, she teeters backwards over the edge of a rift. I snatch at her coat sleeve as she fights for balance. Her pixie boots slither on the crumbling lip, but somehow I haul her into an embrace.

Over her shoulder, twenty metres below, I see the wolves circling on the desert floor.

We look at each other, not daring to breathe for a few moments, waiting for the town to collapse. But it is stable, for the moment.

Kelly lets forth a torrent of abuse peppered with words I have heard only from the denizens of Marfa's saloon. Finally, she says, 'OK, let's bail outta this goddamn town.

Never could bear the place anyhow.'

Luis and I retrieve our horses – I am sure they would have bolted if they weren't so exhausted.

'We do not have much time,' I say, looking at the lights all down the road as they dim or die. 'There is a power here holding the town in the air, but I think it is failing. This is an aspect of the Zone.'

'The wolves, Megan . . .' Kelly says.

'We need to waylay them somehow.' It is difficult to see what we can do. Neither horse is in a state for another gallop, certainly not with Kelly in the saddle as well. We cannot even descend to the ground safely unless it is by the hill . . .

'Denny's,' announces Kelly decisively. She nods towards the restaurant.

'What?'

'I went there some hours back to rustle up some eggs and grits . . .'

I stare at her blankly, thinking she has relapsed into abductee madness.

'The place is full of meat. Bucket-loads of bacon and steak.'

I start to see her drift. Luis smiles and nods.

There is no point in talking it through – we all charge across the street, through the glass doors. There are still jackets over chairs, plates of half-finished food. We follow Kelly's lead, ransacking the kitchen, piling through the refrigerators, clawing anything edible into every container we can find – grated cheese, fries, buns, slabs of raw meat, eggs, bags of burger mince . . . It's all fresh or frozen – preserved all these years since Valentine was ripped clean off the map.

In the forecourt there's a stray shopping cart from the 7-Eleven. We load up but Kelly grabs the handles from me.

'Water the horses. I'll take care of this.'

'Be spare with the bait until you reach the far end of the town,' I warn. 'Just enough to lure them all with you.'

'Hey, I ain't a retard! I'll be back in ten minutes.'

She takes a running leap onto the wheel guards of the cart and trundles it along the twisted camber of the main street, scattering diner ingredients in her wake and, shouting, 'Here, doggy, doggy. Come'n'get it you mangy critters!'

I am not at all sure how we will all get off, but for now the most important thing is water for the horses. Cisco is lathered up with foam and licking at some spilled juice in the front entrance of Denny's.

Luis says, 'She cannot come. She will be a danger. In the *Zona*, it is hard just for us . . .'

'I know. We'll take her to the Deadline border, near Fort Davis, so she can head off-Zone.'

Behind the restaurant is the water tower Kelly spoke of. It is leaning precariously to one side and the ladder that leads to its steel tank has twisted so badly that the rungs are broken. There is nothing else for it. I check the chambers of the Colt. I have two rounds left.

If anyone is out on the plain, they'll hear the shot. But it can't be helped. Besides, the strange grey cloud that drew us here no longer obscures the town – these hovering streets will be in clear view from anywhere on the southern edge of the Davis Mountains. We will have company soon enough.

All these thoughts tumble through my mind as I line up the shot and fire. A spurt of water gushes free and soaks us. I fill up my hat for Cisco but after a while there's no need because the hollow under the tower becomes a pool.

Very soon, though, the tank shudders and tips away from me and a line of lamp posts drops out of sight. It's agonising but we wait for the horses to take their fill, while I stock up my calfskin containers, then lead them back to the front of Denny's. Over the edge of the broken road there's no sign of the wolf pack, so Kelly must have lured them all away.

What's nagging at me is this: even if one of the horses could leap back onto the hill, with two of us in the saddle the burden will be too much to sustain much more than a trot after that. We'll be easy prey if the wolves pick up our trail again as they surely will.

Another chunk of the town bottoms out as Kelly comes running up the main road. I hear it crashing to the ground in waves. She yells something and as I swing up onto Cisco, she pulls me back.

'The car,' she gasps.

'What?'

She retches into the kerb. 'We'll take the car. It's the only way . . .'

Luis shakes his head in admiration. '*Bien pensado!*'

For the first time today, I smile. Because I have

dismissed Kelly and that is a poor judgment. Her thinking is clearer than mine. If we go in the police vehicle, then both horses will be unencumbered. They can last the journey, and Luis and I can keep the wolves at bay with rifles while Kelly drives. It might be desperate, but it is still a plan at least.

Kelly slings me her rifle and jumps into the driver's seat. Luis takes up position in the back. I dither a moment, because it is a long time since I have sat in a motorised transport.

'Sweet baby Jesus, are you gonna strap in or stand there admiring the ride?'

Cisco pads about in a worry, but I'm sure he will catch the gist once we start moving.

I flop into the seat. It feels too close to the road. Through the windshield I see only the crown of the hill.

'Will you be able to drive it across the gap?' I have no idea what this vehicle is capable of.

'Sure. Just put your belt on, will you, goddamn it?'

'Rapido, Kelly!' cries Luis.

Kelly turns the engine on, and looks at me. There is a reckless glint in her eye.

'Always wanted to do this.'

'What?' I ask. The truth is I am a little shaken by the crooked death-wish smile she throws me.

'Road trip, honey. You ready?'

But she does not wait for me to answer. As I slot the belt into its holster, she slams the vehicle into a forward momentum, flips the sunglasses down over her eyes and lets out a long whooping scream.

The bonnet seems to suck up what remains of the road as I am thrown back into my seat. And then there is no more road. We are airborne.

THE DEADLINE
SETTLERS

Airborne. But not for long!

The vehicle tips and crunches nose-down into the hill. Everything loose inside hurtles forward and clatters into the dashboard – cardboard cartons of pizza, coffee cups, a storm of papers. Miraculously, the belt I clicked into its holster holds me firm or I would certainly have been thrown through the glass. The car slides sideways down the slope as Kelly wrestles with the steering wheel.

'Stop it!' I cry.

'Don't you think I'm tryin'!' she yells back.

She levers up the brake and we skid half-circle to a halt. Luis and I stagger out with our rifles, waiting for the dirt to settle. More corners of the town are toppling, buildings leaning into the drop. The road above us has been twisted upwards like a rollercoaster ramp. I cannot see Cisco though I scream to him above the detonations of masonry.

The first of our horses to leap is the Appaloosa. He lands heavily but rights himself on the slope and Luis is there to settle him.

I wait for Cisco. No sign. *Come on!*

I see only blood-red clouds of dust drifting over a web of suspended roads. The lines of tarmac wobble and snap. Perhaps my beloved horse has already fallen. Perhaps he has no heart for the final jump that will bring him to safety. But then, just when I have given up hope, I see an outstretched shape flit across the sun. Cisco!

He jolts down onto the hilltop and slithers out of control, legs splayed, shouldering into the scrub. For a ghastly instant I lose sight of him, but then he appears at the top of a rise, shrugging off the dirt, looking to and fro for me.

I scramble up to him, peering on all sides for wolves, but they have either fled or been crushed by the town.

Cisco nuzzles my hands, sneezing and whinnying softly. I check him over in a panic, but apart from a few cuts and scrapes he is sound, thank the Lord.

Highway 17 is not far. Luis and I lead the horses at a brisk walk alongside the car, northwards towards the Davis

Mountains, keeping a watch for rogue wolves. Kelly grins at us through the open window as the vehicle scrapes onto the highway. It is severely battered and the axle makes a grinding noise that suggests it is coming to the end of its useful life.

Sure enough, with maybe two miles to go to Fort Davis, the engine gives out a sigh of steam and clunks dead.

Luis throws me a glance. I know what he's thinking. Now that we have escaped Valentine, we must surely part ways with Kelly. This is Zone logic – the only sensible course. I wanted to avoid Fort Davis, but we cannot send her cross-country out of the Zone from here – she has no understanding of the dangers. Even with outlaws at large, her safest option is to stay within sight of the Alpine Road until she has crossed the Deadline border.

'So much for the road trip,' groans Kelly.

'It would not have lasted anyway,' I answer. 'All machines break down eventually in the Zone.'

'How come?'

'No one knows for sure. Pa said this place is subject to different laws of the physical world. Machines are too fragile for the forces at play.'

'You mean forces that hold whole towns in the sky?'

'I have heard many unnatural stories of the Zone, but never any that involved such defiance of gravity.'

We abandon the car. For some time, she walks beside us, glancing in my direction, scuffing her toes in the sand. It is clear that she is worried about the situation, but she does not speak until we are in sight of the first tin shacks of sharecroppers, abandoned now on the edge of Fort Davis. Kelly stares at the patchwork of dusty fields, the old irrigation channels that still twinkle with mirrors to corral the sun's rays.

'Hellfire, I sure don't remember it being this way before,' she says.

'The farms? Everyone has to grow their own food around here now – it is too expensive to import from Canada above the Zone. Up there, the sun is stronger, in the west, but mostly their crops go to the edge of the dark side. The prices are prohibitive for us.'

'You can grow stuff in this desert?'

'We have water piped from Brewster County. The sun should be too weak here but there are strains of corn and some vegetables that manage – Zone mutations. Off-Zoners would never eat the food we harvest – they say it has a toxic effect on the mind. But it is edible – just hard to raise and the yields are meagre.'

'God, it's like I recognise things but they been all mussed up, turned inside-out . . . like when Dorothy's house gets dumped from Kansas to Oz, you know?'

It's not long before we spot the watchtowers and scattered coils of barbed wire that lie just east of Fort Davis.

'That the Deadline border you was saying about?'

'Used to be. It was fenced off and guarded for the first year after Visitation, but the edge of the Zone keeps shifting. It is like a tide, claiming and receding from towns. Fort Davis is currently in the Zone, abandoned now, and Marfa is just outside, but a year back it was the other way around. They are both borderline places – any technology more sophisticated than a revolver or a steam-driven pump will not function until you reach places further east like Fort Stockton.'

Kelly stops and stares at the desolate approach. 'How can you tell where the Zone starts and ends then?'

'The only outward signs are scrapped machines. You feel the effects of the Zone in your mind if you're attuned.'

I glance at Kelly's pre-Visitation fashion statements. 'You will attract the wrong kind of attention with those clothes.'

Kelly cocks her head at me. 'So how do I fit in with the locals – does everyone dress rodeo bumpkin and talk like a Bible-thumper?'

'Perhaps we will find some garments for you in Fort Davis – the sharecroppers left in a hurry and did not take all their belongings.'

It is telling, I think, that Kelly has not asked us what our business is in the Zone. She is acting somehow as if she is coming with us when I have tried to explain that we will direct her off-Zone to Fort Stockton. Although I have known her just for a short time, I will be sorry to say goodbye, but she cannot come with us. It is out of the question – all my Zone sense tells me so.

It is quiet as we enter the town. There is a sorry air to the place – home now to mice and undisturbed shadows. We cradle our rifles at the ready. My quivers sense no immediate threat from the Zone but we must be mindful of outlaws. The only sound comes from bats on the wing leaving their roosts in cabin eaves.

'It's evening now?' asks Kelly.

I show her my pocket watch – a quarter before seven. A little crescent moon on the dial indicates that we are after midday, approaching the time of night.

She points at the bats. 'But how do they even know it's time to get going? When the sun never moves.' I think she speaks partly to cut the tension between us. As if she's pretending we will not be parting ways in a matter of minutes.

'Birds, bats, wolves, people – they just adapt, take their cues from each other. We still need sleep. It's just that the sun's rising and setting no longer marks these rhythms.' I sound like a schoolmarm but it settles my nerves somewhat to speak. 'The Earth still revolves around the sun once a year, so there are seasons to speak of, when we are closer to or further away from the light and heat.'

Kelly shakes her head. 'It's all broke to hell. I mean, bats – ain't they needing the night? So how come they don't just flit off to wherever it's dark all the time?'

I watch the empty doorways, the broken shutters – the town ahead is lifeless.

'No food,' answers Luis. 'No insect on the dark side. *Nocturne permanente*. Is too cold. Bats hunt here in twilight places.'

'But how?'

I shrug. 'They have to. Sonar works just as well in light as in darkness.'

'So, the world stops turning and things just go on the same as ever?'

I stop and stare at her then, my abductee pupil, and I'm

astonished for a moment that she is clueless about this. 'Kelly, two and a half billion people perished. Hundreds of millions were displaced. Thousands of species were wiped out. Entire continents are in darkness and ice age. What you see here is what's left.'

Her face turns ash-white. Behind her eyes I watch realisations sink in. There is a world of sorrows beyond her crash-landed town. Perhaps this is the moment her grip on reality will start to crumble, as it is expected for abductees. I am, after all, not trained as a handler.

But at last she nods. 'Just checking.'

We cut across the town away from the main drag, towards the Alpine Road. Just at the edge of the cemetery, I spot a wagon. It is of a type favoured by Deadline settlers – made from scavenged vehicle parts. They usually travel in family groups up and down the border, combing deserted towns for things they can trade. The chassis leans to one side where one of the tyres is flat. A tattered tarpaulin clings to the hooped frame above, snapping in the breeze.

I cup my hand and call out. There is no reply.

'Think they're asleep inside?' I ask.

Luis shakes his head and points at a trail of belongings that seem to have spilled from the back of the wagon – clothes and tools and scrap metal. Kelly picks up a poncho, a hat and a neckerchief. Leaving a wide berth, we edge towards the front of the wagon. Then Luis puts a hand on my shoulder.

'There!' he hisses.

Hidden in shadow between the empty team poles I see

several figures. They are all kneeling, heads bent forward, as if praying.

'Hello?'

No answer.

'I really don't like,' whispers Luis.

'Me neither.'

I sniff at the air, and there is no smell of blood or death but I already know there is nothing to be done for them.

'We should go,' I decide.

'Shouldn't we check at least?' hisses Kelly. 'There's kids there. We can't just ride on and leave them.'

'They're dead, Kelly.'

'How come they're kneeling like that?'

It's not until we are ten paces or so from them that all doubt is removed. The patch of ground around them is frozen, ice crystals twinkling in shadow. Their hands dangle from sleeves stiff with frost. Mini-icicles hang from their hair. A man, a woman and two children no older than five.

'Jesus!' breathes Kelly. 'It ain't that cold, huh? What in hell happened to them?'

Their eyes gaze at the ground, and they are white as cataracts.

SINKHOLES OF
THE MIND

We stare at the family in silence. It hits me then, in that moment, a feeling so sudden and raw, about my family – my mother long dead, Pa missing, and now my aunt shot down in cold blood. The hurt is a shock – why do I feel these things now, after they have happened? These dead pioneers are nothing to me, and yet seeing them I feel my own loss, as if it is fresh. I glance at the others – perhaps Luis will be thinking of his own family all slaughtered, and Kelly of those loved ones she last saw at Valentine, abducted, probably dead.

Luis steps towards the frozen bodies.

'Don't touch them!' I cry.

Luis throws his hands up, annoyed. 'Hey, *calma*! I only look!'

'Don't even step onto the ice.'

'You figure that's Zone handiwork?' asks Kelly.

The sight of the dead children is awful. It is as though they waited for death to come . . . *Why are they kneeling?* They begged, even prayed for their lives.

'Not the Zone. Visitors,' I answer at last.

'What? You mean, the aliens?'

'They are in the guise of outlaws. The Jethro Gang. They are trying to find me.'

'You sure is them?' asks Luis.

'You're being hunted by aliens?' Kelly is for a moment incredulous. But then it is as if she registers all the other madness that has happened to her today. She looks at the clothes in her hands – the clothes of dead people. I think she will drop them in disgust, but she wraps the poncho around her shoulders with a dignity I do not expect of her.

I peer in all directions – across the windblown cemetery towards the town and back the way we have come.

Luis bends to the dirt by the side of the road. 'Many tracks, Megan. Riders, they stop here . . .'

'Christ, how many of 'em are we up against here?' says Kelly.

'Which direction?'

'Is hard to see. I think they split. Some north through graves, some south maybe back to Marfa. Is not so clear.'

73

'We have to get to the mountains, away from the roads.'

'Damn right,' says Kelly. 'There's dozens of packhorse trails up there . . .'

I turn to her. 'You cannot come with us.'

'What? You're gonna leave me here?'

'I told you we would direct you off-Zone.' I put my rifle into her hands and fetch her a calfskin of water from my pack. 'Keep in sight of the roads but not on them – once you reach Alpine over the border it will be safe enough for you. From there you can get a bus further east . . .'

'Hey, so that's it? You're just gonna dump me on a Greyhound? *Adios* and good luck?'

I point at the settler family, as still as stones. 'Kelly, Visitors *killed* those people. If I had to guess, they were questioned first. About me. About whether they'd seen me come through here.'

'I ain't running off to Alpine or Fort Stockton or wherever.' She stands her ground, glaring at me.

'You don't understand . . .'

'No, *you* don't understand! If my folks is any place it's in this crazy-ass country, this *Zone*. So I'm staying while there's still a chance they're alive out here.'

Luis shakes his head. 'Is dangerous for you, is dangerous for us. It is like *tormenta* in the Zone . . .'

'Yeah, but you ain't leaving it, are you? So I ain't, neither. Goddamn it, you owe me! If it's so dangerous here, you can show me the ropes. Three heads are better than one.'

Three. A remnant of that flash migraine blurs my mind

for a moment. *What is it about three?* Maybe Kelly needs to be with us. But taking a novice – it's too risky.

'I'm not listening to this.' I mount Cisco. 'I told you fair and square when we met – you cannot come, we have urgent business to attend to.'

'Like what? How come you ain't leaving the Zone anyhow?' she challenges.

'I have neither the time nor the inclination to tell you about our private affairs.' It comes out colder than I was aiming for.

'Well, 'scuse me for asking, Miss High'n'mighty. The way I see it you got the time but not the trusting.' She marches off ahead of me and it's clear she's dead-set on heading straight into the mountains, with or without us.

Luis looks at me and shrugs. We can't very well force her to leave the Zone. I hang back for a moment, feeling bad, watching all the anger and hurt in the way she strides.

'Wait up, Kelly. I'm sorry. Look, if we could help you we would.'

She whirls to face me. 'I know you think I'm dead-weight'n'all. That I'm out my depth here. But I was offering to help you, team up. Whatever it is you're up to. When I know what I need to about Zone surviving then I'll be out of your hair.'

That throws me. It is clear she is determined to head into the Zone. But if she goes alone she will be dead within a day . . .

'Not a little tempted?' she asks. 'Figure we all did pretty good getting off Valentine in one piece together.'

I wonder if we would have been stranded on the falling ruins had it not been for Kelly and her vehicle skills.

'I believe you are a worthy partner,' I begin. 'But we, Luis and I, are looking for my father missing these last two years.'

Two years since I saw him. I smart at the sting of his absence as if it were yesterday. He told me to leave those three kestrel eggs be. He showed me how to use his camping stove. He used to hate my aunt's bible readings. I thought I had forgotten those things.

Kelly stares at me.

'Our paths are not the same,' I mutter at last.

'How do you know? I'm looking for my family, same as you. Maybe your pop is one them abductees . . .'

'He's not. He is alive and well somewhere out there, and I mean to find him.'

'What makes you so sure he's alive?' Her question is not unfriendly.

'Virgil Bridgwater is the most respected tracker of the entire Zone – no one knows it like he does.'

'*Destino*,' mutters Luis at my side.

Destino – fate. I do not believe in fate, but many trackers including Pa consider the Zone to have a *purpose*. And it acts, it is said, in mysterious fashion – it is in general hostile but there are stories, rumours really, that benign forces operate here too. Perhaps fortune occurs only to lull the unsuspecting traveller, to lure him to destruction. But, still . . . A tracker should be alert to all Zone happenings, good or ill.

I stare at Kelly then. Is it more than mere coincidence

that we have come across her? She has appeared on our path after an abduction twenty years ago. Why now? The wolves, it could be argued, drove us into the gloom that obscured the town from view. And I think also about what my aunt said – how the Visitors mean to take this world from us. If she is right, then how would it benefit Kelly to flee east? I planned to come into the Zone alone. But now I have companions – first Luis, then Kelly. We three . . .

'I know my father is alive,' I say to her at last. 'He may know how to save us, if we can find him.'

'Save us?'

'The Visitors surely seek to overrun all these habitable lands, to take this world for their own kind.'

'Can't we put up a fight? I mean, how many of them are there?'

'No one knows. They show themselves only rarely. But perhaps the true threat has not revealed itself yet.'

'What do you mean?'

'The sun and the Earth are . . . moving. To some new destination.'

'What? How?'

'It is a mystery. There have been three jumps since Visitation. We cannot tell from here because the sun is still too bright. But on the dark side there have been new configurations of the stars. They happened in the blink of an eye. We are streaking through the heavens in leaps and bounds.'

I wait for her to absorb this news, watching as she begins to imagine what this might mean, what horrors.

'And we're going where?'

I shake my head. 'After each jump it takes months to pinpoint our new position in the Milky Way.'

'Dragged to the slaughter, eh? To wherever they're all at.'

'It's what most people believe.'

'How long we got?'

Luis shrugs. 'One year? One hundred? Tomorrow?'

'And your pa, what does he believe?'

I tell her then, about him disappearing into the Zone to search for its secrets, the scrawled map that may lead us to him, the outlaw Visitors on my trail who murdered my aunt, our escape from Marfa.

For some while, she is silent, perhaps in shock at the world she has arrived so suddenly into. It is clear that nothing is how she remembers it.

I show her the map. 'The Mavis Pilgrim is a stagecoach route – it is important somehow. But these other places, this graveyard, these rocks – I know nothing of them.'

'You mean you don't know where you're headed?' She looks at us in mild disbelief.

'Not exactly,' I admit. 'The stagecoach route is north of here between the towns of Hope and Truth or Consequences. There is a tracker at White Sands, a man experienced in the ways of the Zone, who may help us decipher the map further.'

She snatches the paper from my hand to peer more closely at it. 'About as clear as algebra,' she mutters.

Luis darts a glance at the wagon as if it may harbour lurking Visitors. 'They maybe come back, Megan.

Vamoose, eh?'

'Wait up,' says Kelly. 'This last one . . .'

'Sun and two rocks,' says Luis flatly. 'Where is this?'

'Not a sun, butt-muncher. A spider. And look – two pillars, one shorter than the other where the cemetery's at, see?'

'So? Without a name it could be anywhere in the Zone.'

She grins at me. 'I been there. Two vacations. Like the first one wasn't boring enough. Hiking with my dad. Why we couldn't go to Disney World like a normal family, I ain't exactly sure. Trailing round in the sun looking at Injun crap that's about a hundred years old or whatever. Boy oh boy, another sacred mountain, gee, another holy burial ground . . .'

'Kelly, just tell us where it is.'

'Spider Rock, Canyon de Chelly, Arizona. Trust me it's a dump.'

Luis smiles. '*Destino.*'

From Cisco's saddlebags I produce my Rand McNally atlas of the Zone. It is fashioned from pre-Visitation road guide pages taped together, filled with notes of what I know about the country ahead.

'Which way, Kimosabe? Hey, I can't believe I'm going back to Spider Rock. Vacation number three . . .'

I face her suddenly, unsure where my temper has come from. 'This is no vacation, Kelly. And you'd better stop thinking it is. We are only at the very margins of the Zone here. We will be fortunate indeed to emerge from this country with our sanity intact, even more fortunate to remain alive.'

I spare a final look for the settler family. We cannot even risk giving them a Christian burial.

'There are not just rattlesnakes and scorpions and outlaws and Visitors here, but sinkholes of the mind. The Zone *preys* upon you – it sows doubt and prejudice and hate and demonic visions. Every step you take from here on in, take it with respect or not at all.'

I wrap up my atlas carefully.

'Does that mean I'm coming?' says Kelly at last.

My outburst is born of fear. Fear that in bringing Kelly along, I am making a foolish mistake, one that a seasoned tracker would never make. But the Zone has given me a message and I cannot ignore it. Perhaps Kelly is the meaning of *three*. And she has earned a chance. I hold out my hand and she swings up into the saddle behind me.

'The deeper into the Zone we go, the more dangerous and unpredictable it will become. You take your lead from me.'

'Roger that. But I gotta tell you, I'm hungrier than Henry the hungry hound here. You got any Hershey bars? Fruit By The Foot? Twizzlers? Man, I could destroy a patty melt. With double fries. Maybe a McFlurry. Do people eat that stuff now? I'll bet there ain't a single wide-load left in America now. Not one. Hey, do you even know what I'm talking about?'

THE INVISIBLE OCEAN

From Fort Davis we ride into the mountains. Their slopes are measled with trees, rising to a sky studded with pink clouds. We trot through dry grasses, past worm-ridden fences collapsing into the undergrowth.

We take it slowly. By the most direct path, Canyon de Chelly is around five hundred miles north-west of us. But it is not simply a matter of following trails, though the trails are plenty. The fastest route to a place in the Zone is seldom the wisest. It would be hard enough if all we had to think about were water and food for both horses and the three of us, weather, terrain, shelter, wild animals, lawless men and Visitors. What worries me most is our lack of Zone experience.

There are special places of unmoving power – by and large known and avoided by trackers of even limited experience. These are marked on my atlas – the accumulated lore of people who have learned the hard way and were fortunate enough to tell the tale. But the Zone as a rule is never fixed. Laid over the conventional charts of hills and valleys, mesas and ravines, rivers and towns, there lies another set of contours. These shift and settle, flow and swirl, like weather fronts – sometimes sluggish, sometimes gathering into storms and floods. An invisible ocean that washes through the minds of men. There are currents to muddy your thoughts, to stir your fears, to sluice away the very essence of who you are.

At the moment, though, my reading of the Zone is quiet – ruling out none of the many different trails that open up before us into the Davis Mountains.

A cold easterly wind brings in damp air and clouds over the escarpments. We rise quickly into the wrinkles between slopes, grasses swishing at the legs of the horses. Bats carve through the air, picking off insects, banking so low you can hear their flight like the hiss of a switch.

We huddle nose-to-tail under darkening cloud, each of us host to private thoughts. Cisco ambles along picking at any succulent growth he can spy – I envy his ignorance of the whole adventure. I have many misgivings, the most immediate of which is that I must sleep eventually, and I am already tired. Kelly hums gently at my back – she has no idea that here she is as vulnerable as a child. I must tell her some things or she may not even last the night. But I have to choose my moment. For now I concentrate solely on vigilance.

I watch mist envelop crags and crevices. I watch the sudden burst of crows from a dead tree. I listen to the furtive scratchings of rodents or snakes in the undergrowth. I smell the red dust and secretions from the torn buds of prickly pear. I touch the heads of grasses as they give way to Cisco's patient plodding. These things are normal. I *monitor* the land for this is the best way to sense a shift in the Zone. There *are* outward indicators, because animals sense these shifts too, but really it is a way to tune your mind, to discipline it. Only then will you be ready when the quivers begin. If you retreat into daydream and comfortable memories, you will be undone.

Of course, daylight remains but there are changes in pitch that herald the night. The call of the saw-whet owl, exactly as the name sounds. A throb of tree crickets. We make it to the head of the Powell Ranch Road by the early hours. By now, Kelly's demands for rest and food are insistent. I cannot blame her – I'm exhausted too.

We make camp.

'I ain't laid my head down since way before you even showed up at Valentine,' she complains. 'It's this damn sundown on freeze-frame – you never know when it's time for bed. How in hell do you put up with it?'

'Bury your head down a hole. Or if you lucky like me . . .' Luis produces his coveted United Airlines eye mask.

'Gimme, gimme! Now you're talking, bro!'

'What you give for it – one night only.'

'Anything. Name it.'

'Cooking *and* cleaning pans. For one week.'

Kelly lays upon him a torrent of good-natured abuse. But he will not budge.

'It ain't worth a week, dude. Two meals max.'

'Nooo. You see. You try sleep with just shawl. Then you pay me *two* weeks! You see.' He flaunts the eye mask, stumbling about the camp in a show of blindness.

'Don't be swindled,' I warn her. 'You'll grow accustomed to the light. Just tie your neckerchief across your brow.'

'Not the same!' he taunts.

A campfire is certainly a risk in open country, where people can spy the smoke from a distance, but here we are nestled in a steep-sided valley with cover from the mist.

Soon we have a little blaze and some coffee brewing, and though it is bitterly cold, our spirits are up. Kelly puts in a down-payment of one meal's preparation for the eye mask. A skillet of beans and bacon bits. We take it in turns to mop up the juice with corn bread.

'I'll take first watch,' I volunteer. 'Luis, you'll have to share with Kelly.'

He nods.

'What? I'll take my turn. I ain't a kid.'

Luis stares into the flames, reluctant to cross swords with anyone, especially Kelly.

'This isn't the same as just staying awake. You must guard against shifts in the Zone as well as physical intruders.'

84

She sighs in a bored way. 'Holler if I see a flying town, yeah?'

'It is considerably more taxing.'

'I was kidding, Megan. Can you really not tell the difference? OK, I'm all ears.'

'You must disappear.'

'What? Now, you're kidding, right?'

Luis smiles, his eyes intent upon me, remembering perhaps when I tried to teach him these tracker skills on small forays at the edge of the Zone.

'No, disappearance is the aim. Metaphorically speaking. Look and listen and smell and touch everything around you. Remember everything you can down to the tiniest detail. That is called setting up a perimeter.'

'You know there really is only one job for you when you grow up. Headmistress . . .'

'You need to be able to picture the perimeter even with your eyes closed. Keep patrolling it in your mind. Not just the outer limit but the whole area you have marked out. It is easier in an enclosed space like this valley, but in open country the wider the perimeter the earlier the warning.'

'Warning – like of what?'

'Animals, winds, smells – they will leave and enter your perimeter. You must just keep them all under scrutiny. Zone dangers are not always apparent in the physical world – in fact the most deadly are certainly not obvious.'

'Then how the hell am I meant to spot them?'

'If you have set the perimeter up correctly, you will *feel* the onset of Zone perils. As a quickening of the heart, or a racing of the mind. Your senses will tell you, even if you cannot articulate what is wrong. You must be outside of petty concerns, the grumbles of your belly, the itch in your toes, or you will not notice the change until it's too late. That is why you must disappear. You must leave your skin behind – *be* out there in the Zone, at least as far as the perimeter.'

'You still ain't said what I'm meant to do if the horrors come knocking. Sure, if a mountain lion sniffs round the horses, I clash pans, wave round a stick, pick up a rifle. But what if I get the heeby-jeebies?'

'Wake me up. Quietly. Quickly. Act on anything you feel is strange. Promise me.'

'What happens when crap meets fan? Then what?'

'I cannot say. No two Zone perils are the same. They may be inside dangers or outside, or both. We can only react. Promise me – dismiss no instinct of fear, however small. False alarms are inevitable.'

'Cross my heart and hope to die. How long's a watch?'

'Three hours. It's hard, but you have Luis – you can share the burden of the perimeter.'

'So if you're travelling on your own, how can you keep an eye on things?'

'The best trackers set the perimeter up and patrol it in their dreams.'

'Eh?'

'I was kidding. They do critter-sleep.'

'They what?'

'Their brains shut down about seventy to eighty per cent. They sleep with their eyes open. With their backs to a wall. Like hunted animals.'

'You mean they don't sleep.'

'They enter a state of semi-consciousness, but their senses are on alert for changes in the perimeter. It is not easy and it is not restful. Trackers age beyond their years. Some go mad from lack of genuine sleep. But it is possible. Horses sleep standing up. Birds sleep on the wing. I am not adept. But I will practise a while when it is your turn to watch.'

As the flames of our campfire haze the air, I set up my perimeter. Kelly grumbles for about one minute about how the sunlight will keep her awake for ever. Then she is instantly asleep, lying in her poncho as if poleaxed.

Luis flicks the elastic on his eye mask. I tell him his bargain with Kelly won't last, that she'll see she's been duped. Sleeping in the Zone is easy – it's staying alert that's hard. He shrugs with a smile, and it is as if we are just camping out on the edge of Marfa – no cares.

'I trust you, Megan. Watch safe.'

Eye mask down, he sings a rambling ditty in Spanish but even before it is finished he too is asleep. I watch him for longer than I should, his gentle breathing, his arms sprawled out on the open ground, and I'm amazed suddenly that he is here, in this wild place, in my care. I enclose Cisco and the Appaloosa into my protective sphere, taking note of their jostling arrangement. Some time into the watch, I have the valley so corralled in detail that I can afford briefly to think of the Sheriff of Marfa. I pray for him to pull through despite the pain he must be suffering.

I rouse the others at four-thirty in the morning, waiting until they are alert enough to take on the watch. I try for the critter-sleep but I am too far gone. I listen to Kelly and Luis, envious of their mild bickering, grateful that they are here with me.

An hour later, Kelly shakes my shoulder. It is a smell that has alarmed them though it has abated. They cannot name it and I cannot pick it up even though I stay awake with them for twenty minutes. The horses do not seem unduly perturbed, although that is no guarantee of safety.

I sleep again. And dream of the shoot-out at the jailhouse. In this version, the sheriff does not come to my rescue. The outlaw Visitor walks through the bars as if they do not exist. And within his eyes I see fires. As distant as bonfire beacons. Pa calls me. But he is far away – not in the jailhouse. He calls from a place where the golden flames live. Not a warning but a beckoning. And I must be quick.

I wake with a terrible start, as if my legs are mid-stride.

Things are instantly wrong.

The perimeter is all out of kilter.

Luis is trying to calm the horses.

Kelly points southwards, the direction we have journeyed from. The sky is a breathtaking black. Impossibly, clouds are spilling in from two opposite sides of the mountain range.

'Ain't no ordinary storm, that's for sure . . .' Her voice is drowned by thunder.

And spiking down from the clouds comes a bolt the

shape of lightning. But it casts no light.

It is black, like a fault in the sky, like a crack to the dark side of the Earth.

THE ONE-WAY VALLEY

'If that ain't hellfire, then I don't know what is.' Kelly is mesmerised, as I am.

I scramble up the scree to get a better view of the storm. It is huge and it is coming this way.

Another black fork tears down the sky. It leaves a mark on your eyesight, like real lightning. Great swathes of rain move across the plain – and at this distance they are truly startling, like the skirts of the Northern Lights, but dark and impenetrable.

I count the seconds to the thunder rolls. They bounce around the peaks like trapped stampedes.

Kelly joins me on the outcrop. 'We gotta get outta here, Megan.'

'What was that smell? Do you remember now?'

'Are you crazy? We've gotta go!' She pulls my arm.

'No, it's important. The smell, Kelly – it was a warning.'

'It weren't nothing. Pretty faint. I only caught it for a moment.'

'Just you, or Luis also?'

'Both of us, same time. I dunno. It was like it didn't belong here. But then it was gone.'

'What do you mean it didn't belong here?'

'Just weren't what you'd expect, I guess. Felt out of place.'

I watch Luis down in the valley floor. He is trying to settle the horses – they jitter about, starting this way and that. The storm dismays them but it has not struck terror into their hearts. Neither are they comforted by Luis, and that feels wrong. They are afraid of something else.

'Isn't it strange that you cannot identify the smell?'

'Jesus, Megan. Are you even awake yet? That storm's gonna be here five minutes tops and it's laying down black light! That reads bad in anybody's book, don't it?'

'We cannot outride it. There is another danger . . .'

'What? Worse than the storm out of Revelations? Can we just go?'

She does not wait for my reply but bounds back down the scree towards the camp.

'Kelly, stop!'

But she either does not hear me, or she chooses not to.

I take one last look at the thunderhead. Zone weather is often outlandish, sometimes deadly. But it is usually a consequence of something else. Threats are oblique here. I try to read my quivers but the messages are crossed, contradictory. It would seem the only sensible course – to flee in the face of such raw and dark power. But . . . my dream of Pa. I have to come to the danger, *to face it*, not to run. The wind kicks up in restless squalls. Curtains of rain cloak the foothills – they are so thick I cannot see through them.

Kelly yells at me from below, frantically waving her arms. Luis is struggling to keep both horses in check. If I was alone I would sit the storm out but things are slipping from my control.

As Kelly sees me leave the outcrop, she breaks into a run towards the horses. All too late I see the true danger. At the campfire we were *three* – watching over each other, strong somehow. But now we have allowed ourselves to be separated.

'Kelly! KELLY!'

She does not heed me. I lose my footing near the tail-end of the slope and crash through the remains of our camp. Tin plates flip up into the wind like giant coins. The storm is already upon us. Flight is pointless.

I yell at them to stop but the wind is deafening, ripping through the valley now, sweeping the grasses flat in violent swirls. Kelly leapfrogs over the hind legs of the Appaloosa and clean into the saddle. It is a reckless way to mount a horse in this weather and it bolts immediately.

Luis holds on to Cisco, just. I watch Kelly barrelling straight down the Powell Road. And I know she's riding headlong into disaster.

I see the whites of Cisco's eyes as I mount him, and for a moment he is crazed – just tossing every which way. Luis roars a question at me that I cannot hear. But it can only be one thing. *Do we follow or not?* My quivers say no. But how can I leave her? Without Kelly I would not even be here.

I help Luis into the saddle behind me, then as we charge away after her, the rain hammers in.

'*Buena decisión*!' he calls out to me. Good call. But is it?

I am sodden in seconds. We have not reached the first bend before I see muddy white torrents spilling over parapets either side of me and filling the road. Forget Revelations, this is Genesis. Another bend, then a longer, flatter stretch. Luis clings to my waist, and yells encouragement to Cisco. Ahead, I can just make out Kelly. Is her horse slowing?

My quivers are going haywire. A wave of rain pummels down so hard I lose sight of everything and in that moment I sense a shift in the Zone. I feel it as a dread worse than the storm – a closing off. We have passed some kind of boundary, a point of no return. The rain thrums into my jacket and turns in an instant to hail – stones the size of cobnuts.

Kelly has pulled up. The Appaloosa circles and shies from the road beyond. As we reach her, the sound of hail becomes truly deafening. Like the mountains above us are being reduced to gravel. I look up and back just in time to see the black lightning up close. It seems to split the valley in two – a vision of night that this land has not seen since Visitation. And as the sky heals up, the rain gives a taste I did not expect. Salt. A mineral tang like cold blood.

Kelly yells above the hail. 'Rotten fish!'

'What?'

'The smell!'

Now I catch it. She points to the ditch alongside the road. It is choked with dead fish – heads and tails and spines that look half-eaten.

Abruptly the hail stops just as Kelly is shouting. 'I DON'T LIKE THIS! LET'S . . . get out of here.'

'We can't – the way back will be barred. I felt it as we came through.'

'What do you mean?'

'Just that!' I snap at her. 'This is a one-way valley. You come in, you can't go back the same way. The horses will refuse. We'd have to leave them here.'

'We can try.'

'We cannot try! I told you to wait but you would not listen. This is what happens when you panic here, when you make rash decisions on your own.'

Luis tugs at my arm.

A great shadow falls over the road.

And from above comes a new sound. Thrashing.

I duck as a salmon hits the road beside me and writhes weakly.

The temptation to look up is unbearable. The thrashing becomes a roar.

'Get down!'

And an avalanche of fish engulfs us.

The road runs silver and red – a seething, thumping torrent of creatures, as though vomited from the heavens. They slap and gape and die in a sliding heap that rises to Cisco's hocks. He is rooted, beset by fears from every direction, slithering in fish guts, bowed by the sheer weight of the deluge.

It lasts for a full minute, then as suddenly as it began, it ends. A few small fry join the massacre. Luis lifts a squid gingerly from his hat. It is his way of brazening out the fear – this comic gesture. A good way, I think. Any distraction is welcome to keep panic at arm's length. The stench is epic – a rising tide of destroyed shoals.

The horses stand stunned.

Kelly stumbles through the sludge of scales and entrails. 'Jumpin' Jesus. Christ.'

She looks at me and laughs.

And something enormous plummets down between us. It splits as it lands, showering us with gunk. We all jump and crouch at the same time, our screams gagging in our throats. A swordfish. Bigger than Cisco.

The horses screech and tear free. They would be gone if they could get a sure footing in all the mess. Poor Cisco raises his head higher and higher in a desperate bid to escape. It takes me a full five minutes to calm him.

'Is this actually happening?' asks Kelly at last.

I pluck up the courage to glance at the sky, just in case there's a whale on the way down. The clouds are dispersing.

Spasms of fear run through me, even as I try to master them. 'It is really happening. And we are still in trouble.'

'You ain't kidding. I hate fish.' She gags at the smell.

'Quiet!' My quivers are at full pitch. *Why is the valley sealed off? Something about the fish.*

Luis draws and cocks his rifle.

'No, wait!'

They lumber in from the slopes, out of shelters and outcrops high above, some leaping and shaking their shaggy pelts. They are starving. They have been waiting. The rotten remains of the last downpour have barely sustained them. Grizzlies. Dozens of them.

They bound into the feast, raking it up in their giant paws. We edge together.

'Don't shoot, Luis. Not unless you have to.'

'Yeah, roger that,' says Kelly. 'Like maybe they ain't too bothered about us, huh?'

A gigantic male pads into the melee. His hide is scored with claw marks – one eye missing. He rears up to his full height and sends out a rasping cry to others. A challenge perhaps? Squabbles break out. We are close enough to hear the clash of teeth, their laboured breathing.

The horses dart and rear, flashing the whites of their eyes. I try to keep Cisco close and call words of comfort to quieten his terror.

My Zone sense is clouded but safety beckons. I feel it in quivers – now that the fish have fallen, the road ahead is clear, just for a while, as the bears sate their hunger.

'Keep together. Move slowly. With me.'

'Let's hope they ain't hankering for a different menu.'

'Is OK. We all smell fish. Not horse. Not human.'

Our retreat is delicate. They know we are here but they are preoccupied with territorial disputes, with gorging themselves on easier pickings. But they are everywhere, and it only takes one to rush us.

The slavering, the bellowing, the crunch of fish heads splitting open. It's too much for Kelly. She hands me the reins to the Appaloosa and heaves over to vomit. To her credit she manages it quietly, then makes a heroic effort to hold the rest of her supper down.

'Holy Moses. It's like all your Fridays at once.'

A matriarch crosses our path.

'You're too close to her cubs!' I hiss at Kelly.

'Hell, I'm just trying to stay away from the big ones!'

'Well don't. She will take us apart if we get too near her young.'

We pull away from the main group and pick up speed as the fish haul thins out. Luis takes the rear, backing up with his rifle primed, but the bears do not follow. A mile further down the road, we reach the storm's limit – just a few fresh herring caught in the branches of trees, like glittering fruit.

Now that the danger has passed, my anger mounts.

'Cod alive! We was nearly kippered there, eh?' quips Kelly.

I don't answer.

'Hey, lighten up, you mullets. Cod be worse . . .'

I round on her. 'Kelly, you nearly got us killed back there.'

'Hey, you led us into these mountains in the first place.'

'Yes, and I would have led us safely out of them again if you hadn't taken matters into your own hands. You never ever just charge off without taking the measure of the Zone around you. Ever.'

'The storm—'

'The storm was not the greater menace! The black lightning, the hailstones, the salt rain – the Zone *wants* you to be scared! Don't you understand? It wants you to lose your head with visions of the Apocalypse. But it is just the displacement of a faraway sea. The Zone does these things. It is what counts as natural in these parts. But the real threat comes from the bears that know the fish are coming.'

'I think I know that already.' Her sulk is tinged with embarrassment.

'But you didn't know it five minutes ago! Did you? The valley is a giant trap. One of the easier ones to predict. And we walked straight into it. The bears could not leave if they wanted to. That's why they are starving. We were lucky it rained when it did or they would have eaten us alive.'

Luis puts his hand on my wrist. Gently. To tell me that I have said my piece.

The lack of an apology smarts. Because we rode after her and she does not realise we had a choice. I stew in a righteous anger for a full ten minutes.

'Megan, look. Hold up. I'm sorry. Really I am.'

It would have been better if we had parted company

with her in Fort Davis. But I say nothing.

'Seriously. I won't hare off again. I'll listen. Teach me, oh Master. No, seriously. I goofed.'

She holds out a hand caked in fish slime.

It *is* pretty funny to see her doused head to foot in fish parts. Someone who detests fish. I'll be damned if I'll let it show but then I can't help myself. And it feels good to let go a little.

Finally I take her hand. She makes a show of not being able to prise our fingers apart.

'Hey, is that a smile, folks?' She looks over her shoulder to an imaginary audience. 'Megan Bridgwater – in severe danger of cracking her face. It's a first, people. And you saw it here. Now, we're rolling! Check it out.'

Luis grins at me like a buffoon. He has a sprat in the breast pocket of his shirt. And my resistance crumbles.

'The whole sea falls out the sky and that's your best catch?' Just for a moment, laughter runs away with my words, and I feel free.

'Can't be a crab your whole life,' says Kelly with a smile. 'We've haddock enough.'

THE JOURNEY TO BROKEOFF

The Powell Ranch Road takes us east to join the head of the Wild Rose Pass. We're too visible from main tarred roads so I'd prefer to steer clear of them. However, it is unavoidable for a stretch of perhaps twelve miles as we skirt round the northern edge of the Fort Davis Mountains. We leave the road as soon as the country evens out, and hug the foothills in a north-westerly slant.

The static position of the sun in the sky may cause confusion for the keeping of time, but in some ways it helps with orientation. In my locale of West Texas and the Mexican border, I am used to using my shadow as a compass to indicate an easterly direction. Of course, this cannot be relied upon for long distances – the further west we go, by tiny increments, the sun will appear to rise in the sky, and eventually, after months of travel, the shadows will shorten and then flip to point westwards. It is a strange prospect to me, that only by embarking on a grand journey will I ever experience those mythical sun positions associated with noon and sunrise. Or indeed the dark side of the Earth where night prevails – a starlit terrain locked in perpetual ice. There are human settlements that cling to the edge of this lifeless territory, but explorers only survive on the dark side for as long as their supplies last.

I am on high alert as we cross I-10 where it intersects with I-20. But the highways are empty and desolate. We encounter only a couple of coyotes patrolling the edge of an old gas station that has long been stripped of any useful glass and metals. Under the canopy where the pumps once stood, there is evidence of a recent campfire.

Luis casts about for tracks away from the road. 'Horses here, I think.'

'Could it be them?'

'I don't know. Not so many. Maybe they split again to look for us.' He turns to Kelly, 'You know how to read animal sign?'

'Only sorta sign I can read is "Exit", buddy. They don't teach that kinda stuff at Taco-Shack-O.'

The country all around us is clear. We have been lucky

to avoid them so far.

'If they're splitting up, it shows they don't know where we're headed. We have to keep moving. Let's get clear of the road.'

We meander north along dry gullies. After another couple of hours we find a water hole fed by a clean brook. It feels good to drink our fill and wash some of the mess from our clothes. Kelly says she smells like a dead hobo in a trashcan. Luis answers her banter with jokes of his own. It is effortless, the way they talk. I listen though I am apart. Always apart.

We travel on, encountering no serious peril for three days. This is the longest I have been in the Zone and it is becoming easier to judge its fickle ways. I am steeped in it, the shifting and the ebbing. Threats approach and retreat, but they do not engage. They are subtle – just dispersing before I can scout them out. As though the Zone is teasing us. Kelly and Luis bandy words and I sometimes join in, but I pay mind to these conversations only because they are within my perimeter, my monitoring of the Zone.

At the brief camps we make, Kelly asks about the Zone. She is stunned at how big it is. I show her on my Rand McNally atlas.

'The territory is bounded here – the West Coast, the Pacific Ocean. And here, up through the Canadian province of British Columbia to the tundra wastes of Alaska. And here, where the Americas join at the narrowest point.'

'The Wild West all over again, huh? Anyone got any

idea what the Zone is, like why it's here and not some-place else?'

'Some trackers believe the Zone is protecting some-thing, or hiding it. Something the Visitors don't want us to find.'

'Can't we just send in an army to root it out?'

'We did. And the entire army disappeared without trace. Look, you can't just blunder in here and force the Zone to reveal its secrets. You can't send in aeroplanes or tanks or scientific instruments. You can't even send satellites high over this land. Machines just don't work here. And people quickly lose their sanity unless they have tracking skills.'

She gazes at the atlas pages, the cities that have been abandoned, the major highways that will over time be overrun by nature.

'So maybe whatever the Zone's hiding – we'll find it in that cemetery at Spider Rock. Canyon de Chelly. In a grave.'

'Maybe. Do you remember a cemetery from your vacation?'

'Nope. Just old Injun graves with busted pots. You could buy all that junk in Rock Springs.'

'Many men die. *Después de la Visita*,' Luis reminds us. '*Zona de Diablo* is one grave, no?'

'What about this Mavis Pilgrim stagecoach?' asks Kelly. 'How's that fit in?'

'I'm not certain, but perhaps we must intercept it for a clue, something we must discover before reaching the cemetery.'

'Like what grave we gotta dig up?'

'Possibly.' It is not the first time I have thought about the cemetery the map refers to, the graves it might contain. My aunt had insisted Pa was still alive, after years of believing him dead. Getting hold of the map changed her mind. Who gave it to her? I banish the idea that the map will lead only to Pa's remains. But perhaps it is true and that only by making the journey will I ever know the truth and lay his memory to rest.

We make steady gains – sixty miles over the three days by my reckoning. We could easily pick up the pace but there are dangers in rushing. At this speed, the wrinkles of the mountains and riverbeds unfold at a safe remove. I can advance my perimeter with growing confidence, ready for any perils that lurk ahead. Luis, too, is becoming more adept at reading the Zone – at times he rides ahead, and the routes he picks are sound. I always pictured this journey as a solitary one like those of all legendary trackers, but how glad I am that he is here! Without his help in navigating, the strain of critter-sleep and constant vigilance would have taken their toll already. But having him with me means more than that – it his companionship that sustains me. We have spent our childhoods wondering about the Zone, telling each other stories and sharing make-believe adventures about this place. Experiencing it without him would have seemed wrong, lonely even.

Sometimes Kelly sings to pass the time. She has a rich fine voice. I tell her I don't know any of the songs.

'That's cos I wrote 'em, honey. And you woulda heard of 'em if the world hadn't gone straight to hell. Saved five hundred bucks for a one-way trip to LA. Put my name in lights. Was gonna drive back in a pink Belair and give the finger to every lame-brain loser in the state of Texas who told me I couldn't do it.'

'*Destino*,' sighs Luis.

'Damn straight. I'da made it to LA, I wouldn't be here now, huh? Bet them East Coast places never did so good come Visitin' Day, right?'

'The few trackers who have been that far in-Zone tell of ghost cities.'

'There you go – lucky break. Chasin' fame'll kill you.' She winks at me and breaks into another song.

Our meals are taken quickly – cans of beans warmed in the embers if I feel that a fire is an acceptable risk, cold if not. In private moments, I pull the burrs from Cisco's mane and whisper nonsense into his twitching ear. The words are just a soft babble, of a tone to comfort him. I sit with a blanket around my shoulders and watch Luis and Kelly curled on their bedrolls, like cocoons waiting to hatch.

At a watering place strewn with boulders, Luis shows me the brands he has found on the Appaloosa. They are fired into the hide high on the neck, hidden beneath tufts of mane. A pair of arched scorpions with their stings poised. It is not a brand I am familiar with.

'A ranch further afield?'

Luis points out older brand marks on its shoulder flanks. 'Tumbling three-stripe – San Jacinto River. Changed hands, see? Is Jethro Gang maybe with scorpion mark?'

'I don't know. I mean, rustlers don't normally brand their horses. They might tamper existing brands so they can sell them on. But this one still has its original mark.'

'The Jethro Gang ain't your regular outlaws,' chips in Kelly.

'But why hide the brand like this?' says Luis.

'Pretty rough and ready too, huh?' Kelly is right – it's like the brand wasn't made with an iron at all, more as though it has been drawn on the hide with a hot wire or something.

It is strange and unsettling. I don't share my thoughts with the others but maybe the Visitors have done something more to the horse than just brand him. Finding the scorpions feels like a warning. Still, we cannot afford to set the horse loose – we will make poor progress with just Cisco between three.

I consult my atlas. We are close to the Guadalupe Mountains.

Kelly points at a place just south of Route 62 marked with a scribble of huts. 'Brokeoff? I ain't never heard of that.'

'It is a new town. One that has arisen since Visitation. There are some doldrums places in the Zone where folk can settle without always being on their guard.'

'Well, thank Jesus. I'm real sick of tinned beans . . .'

'We will be avoiding Brokeoff. I do not want to draw attention. Besides all Zone towns are rough and lawless places.'

'Are you kidding? We're all baked here. You ain't laid down in days.'

'Is true,' agrees Luis. 'Maybe news of Mavis Pilgrim stagecoach, eh?'

He gives me an exhausted smile and it nearly sways me – what harm will one night do? But I must be strong.

'It's too dangerous. Even if the Jethro Gang aren't there, Brokeoff is still a wretched hive of murderers and gamblers.'

'They got hotels?' asks Kelly.

'Megan, is good place for supplies, no?'

'Hey, I'm choosing this time,' says Kelly. 'If I eat another goddamn bean I'm gonna hurl.'

'We're not going,' I insist.

'Two to one.'

It is true that our canned goods will not last the journey. And I look again at my companions – they are practically asleep on their feet, the horses too. I don't have the heart to keep pushing them. Rest outweighs risk.

'All right, but we stick together and we keep our heads down.'

Kelly pumps her fist. 'Baths all round, people. And feather beds. And all-you-can-eat . . .'

I have not been to Brokeoff or any Zone settlement, but I cannot imagine it will match Kelly's expectations.

THE DRUNKEN STEER

I am right – the main drag of Brokeoff Town has little to write home about. The silence from Kelly is telling. Even I am disappointed. It is a ramshackle affair – one-storey cabins and tents, corrugated lean-to shelters and trailer homes that sag to one side as though hurled there by hurricanes. Doors bang in the wind. Feral dogs beset by mange lie flaked out in the dust. The boardwalks are in ill repair and serve as shelter for a number of desperate-looking families. The children all wear smocks and hard frowns, and squat in the street to make their ablutions.

'Jeez, why don't they come abduct this crap-hole?' mutters Kelly. 'Be doing them a favour.'

We skirt around mules and goats too tired to move.

Luis asks someone in Spanish for the nearest hotel. The man, a vaquero in a stained straw hat and a Pueblo blanket of red and brown bands, stares at us for a long time before gesturing towards the only building with more than one storey. It looks like an old barn for livestock, but there is a balcony and a saloon bar entrance, and above the swing doors hangs a crooked steer's skull.

The vaquero says something I cannot understand. Even from here I can smell the liquor on his breath. He holds out a grubby hand flecked with blood.

'He says the Drunken Steer is too much dollars,' announces Luis. 'He says we stay with him for less.'

Kelly snorts. 'Yeah, well tell him it's a hell of an offer but if that's the classiest place in town, I say we stick with it. No offence.'

We tie up the horses and push into the saloon. Some cowhands are at the bar drinking from cloudy bottles. One of them is trying to pick out a tune from an upright piano so warped and dusty I figure a merry refrain will cause it to collapse. A card game is in progress in the far reaches of the gloom – serious by the looks of it, for the players do not look up from their cards as we enter.

A large woman tends to the bar. She wears girlish pigtails though she is perhaps fifty years old. Her considerable bulk is barely contained by a frilly polka-dot dress. She does not smile as I approach, just scratches the sores on her elbows and rearranges the holsters on her hips.

Her handguns are the largest I have ever seen – like blunderbusses. It is clear she is the boss.

'We'd like a room, please.'

'And a bath,' adds Kelly.

'And food,' chips in Luis.

She shuffles out from behind the bar to take a closer look at us. Her feet are bare. Her legs are those of a man, sturdy and thick with hair.

'A room *and* a bath *and* food.' She glances at the cowhands who snigger into their bottles.

One of them makes a show of pinching his nostrils. 'Poo-ee, sure figure they be wanting that bath, Josie!'

'You don't smell so good yourself, mister,' snaps Kelly.

The cowhand splutters on his drink and slams down the bottle spoiling for a fight. Luis moves to intercept him, but Josie beats him to it. She fells the man with one devastating punch. The cowhands make no move to pick up their companion and they quickly settle down.

'Well now, you'll have to share a bed. I got the one room left.'

She waits, daring me to object. It throws me that we'll all be bedding down together but what did I imagine – three luxury suites? Besides we've been side-by-side each other in the wilderness for nearly a week . . .

Josie has a wry look on her face – as if taking me for a prude.

'How much?' I ask hastily.

'Four bucks a night – twenty-six for the week. Bath's down the hall. Two nickels for water, dollar for hot. We got a pot of coney on the go. That's on the house.'

I have no idea what coney is. I look at the others. They nod.

'We just need the one night.'

'Suit yourself, Sister. There's a stable out back.' She tosses me a key. 'Show that to Hodges. He'll see your horses right. Don't speak none to him. He's deaf and dumb, and he gets mad if you try conversin'.'

We take the horses to Hodges. The man is a lantern-jawed giant who looks like he could strangle a moose but he's gentle with Cisco.

The room is not as bad as I feared. It is a minor mystery how the good iron bedstead has arrived here in this gritty town. The linen is a little musty but a month of Sundays cleaner than me. I lay down on the mattress, too tired to wash.

'The provisions . . .' I murmur. Already the soft downy bedclothes are lulling me into slumber.

'Don't worry. Me and Luis'll take care of that. But first things first.'

'What are you doing, Kelly?' My voice seems far away.

'What do you think I'm gonna do? I'm gonna scrub up so I don't stink like a cat's dinner and then I'm gonna stuff myself stupid with coney, whatever the hell that is.'

'Just stay out of trouble, Kelly. Stick together, OK?'

'No, I figured I'd get all fancied up and take old Hodges out on the town. I'm kidding.'

Strangely, I feel as though I continue speaking with Kelly. But I have no recollection of the words. My dreams come in a jumbled race, falling one over the other. I am in a stagecoach with Pa – we're trundling through a vast cemetery. He stares out the window watching the graves go by. The stagecoach pulls up and I follow his gaze outside. Only one grave remains – freshly dug. When I turn back, Pa has gone. I am alone cradling a scorpion in the palm of my hand. I should be scared but I'm not. It stings my finger and a single drop of blood wells up from the tip. And as it runs into a dribble it catches fire.

I wake with a start – groggy and uncertain where I am. The last dream lingers. It has the urgency of a message, nagging me to decipher it. I must go to the cemetery by stagecoach? The Mavis Pilgrim perhaps? There is just one grave that matters. A new one. My father's? He was in the stagecoach before he disappeared. I cling to the memory of his face, serious but strangely untroubled. Perhaps the message is *from* him, which would mean he is alive. Maybe he watches over me somehow on this journey. I think of the flash migraine at Fort Davis – the visions of three that helped me decide to bring Kelly with us into the Zone. Visions that all featured Pa in some way.

Then I remember the scorpion but this part of the dream makes little sense. Do scorpions even draw blood? It represents the Visitors? Why wasn't I scared?

My train of thoughts is broken as Luis comes into the room. He thrusts a warm clay bowl into my hands. There is a rich gamey smell from the steaming juices.

'Coney?'

He grins and hands me a spoon.

One mouthful turns into several in quick succession. I have to force myself to slow down.

'Is gophers.' He makes ears with his fingers. 'Is good.

The cook is Josie's daughter. I think I love her.'

I nearly choke. My head races forward in the space of a second to his marriage with this unknown girl – me bravely congratulating them before continuing my journey alone. Then I realise he's joking. 'Josie will string you up,' I laugh, wondering what her daughter looks like.

'I can stay here,' he says with mock hurt. 'Brokeoff is fine town. I will hunt coneys and never shoe horses.'

I look at him, mid-mouthful. There is resolve in his expression that I have not noticed before – a glitter of hunger in his eye. And I realise that anywhere on this Earth, even here in the desperate sanctuary of Brokeoff, in the depths of the Zone, is preferable to Marfa. He has been waiting, with just as much longing as I, to be free of that Deadline town, to come at last into the Zone.

I have held his gaze too long. 'Thanks for coming with me,' I mutter at last, unsure why I feel suddenly agitated. Weren't we just joking a moment ago? But the thought that Luis can choose whichever path he wants – it unsettles me.

He mumbles something in Spanish I don't catch. He takes a deep breath as if set to say something important. But instead he looks at the window, and only then do I notice the rain. It pummels the roof, and lashes the glass in squalls. One decent sleep in this haven from the Zone and all my awareness skills have deserted me. My perimeter just reaches as far as a bowl of gopher broth and my childhood friend.

His face has become troubled. 'Megan . . .' he begins.

What is he going to say? A queasiness takes me as all

his possible confessions come to me at once. *Does he really mean to stay in Brokeoff? Has he changed his mind about travelling further? Has he fallen in love with Kelly?*

Through the floorboards I hear raised and angry voices.

'Kelly! Where's Kelly?'

'I . . . I not see her. In the tub for hours singing . . .'

I trip over my boots. Someone has taken them off for me.

We both run down the hall but the bathtub is empty.

More fierce argument erupts from the saloon below us.

I stumble down the stairs, boots in hand, and stop dead.

It is a sight that cuts the clamour in one stroke – Kelly, steaming from the rain, strides into the saloon leading the snorting Appaloosa across the floor.

I feel certain Josie will intervene and throw us out of her establishment. But the landlady just shakes her head with a half-smile.

Kelly hushes the horse down. She still has her poncho but she is wearing a new black hat, clean jeans and fancy boots with polished spurs. *How long have I been asleep – a week?* It is clear I have some catching up to do.

'Kelly!'

She throws me a warning glance – *don't interfere*, it says.

'I give her dollars for supplies,' Luis mutters angrily to me. 'Not rodeo clothes.'

She ignores us, ties the horse to a post and takes her place at a card table – eight men, all smoking cigars, stare at her. One of them, a man with a sheriff's badge, though he seems far too old to have survived the position of sheriff here, pours her a drink. Kelly throws it back with gusto, coughing only slightly at the strength of it.

Belatedly, I see that Kelly is playing and that a game is in progress. A somewhat alarming pile of dollar bills and casino chips sits mid-table. There are three cards face-up by the pot – the king of diamonds, the ten of diamonds and the queen of diamonds. It is a game I have witnessed at the Welcome Saloon in Marfa – a game that regularly ends in bloodshed. Texas hold'em poker.

Kelly thumbs up the edge of her two face-down cards in the hole – I presume to check they have not been tampered with in her absence.

A red-faced man with a warty nose stands and leans on the table. 'This is most irregular, Miss Tillman,' he says.

'The hell it is, Mr Hart.'

For God's sake, they know each other's names!

'If you cannot see or raise,' he addresses the other players in a patronising tone, 'then you must either check or fold.'

'I know the rules, buddy. I'm just proving to you I got the funds.'

She isn't just gambling with our money, it seems to all the world as though she's losing it. Restraining my anger, I stride up to her. 'Kelly!'

She ignores me, waiting for Mr Hart's response. The man throws me a nasty look, warning against interference. He seems smug about his hand and wants the game to conclude.

'Well, what is your play?' he drawls. 'I think we're all dying to know.'

'Josie, what's my horse worth?' asks Kelly, without taking her eyes off Hart.

Josie ambles up to the Appaloosa, checks his teeth and feels his legs. 'Two fifty. Two seventy with the saddle.'

'Three hundred and twenty,' says Kelly.

'Two eighty-five,' counters Josie.

'What the hell. I'm gonna be buying him back in five minutes. Done.'

Luis draws a sharp breath at the recklessness of the deal, and mutters an oath in Spanish. Where we come from, horse-trading takes days.

'Fats, pay the girl,' orders Josie.

The dealer, a man that in no way could be described as fat, peels off the money in fives and tens.

I hover by the table, desperate to put an end to the game, but what can I do? I'm not playing – I'm just a spectator.

'Kelly,' I breathe. 'This is insane.'

She slaps fifty dollars into the pot. 'See you and raise you.'

The player to Kelly's left – a shifty-looking man with bad acne and sporting a pair of mirror sunglasses – blanches and folds his hand. Two more check with a nonchalant tap of the knuckles. Much tutting and wry shakes of the head. Around the table, the betting continues – fold, fold, call. The dealer burns and lays another card face-down into the flop. Queen of hearts. A few sharp intakes of breath. Some more onlookers gather round the table.

'Kelly . . .'

She turns to me sharply. 'What are you, my mother? I can't walk away now else I'm stuck in this tin-can town for ever.'

Fury swells into me – a rush of blood so rapid I want to beat her. For being so selfish, for jeopardising our mission, for her vanity, her pride, her pig-headed stunts. Only a hand on the shoulder from Luis stops me from giving into rage. It's just as well, a raised fist now, in the middle of this poker game, will start a riot. But I swear, if she loses I'll land one on her so hard she'll be needing what passes for a dentist in Brokeoff.

It is Hart's turn to begin the betting. He places fifty in the pot with an unnecessary flourish, though there is a layer of sweat above his lip for all to see.

Kelly raises another fifty without hesitation. The players to her left fold in disgust. Their discarded hands show a lack of diamonds. Only Hart and Kelly remain – perhaps one of them is hoping for a royal flush that beats all. The dealer burns and deals the river. It is a lowly three of spades.

Kelly leads the betting with everything she's got left. All in.

'*Madre Maria!*' Luis takes a pace forward and every customer in the saloon glares at him.

Hart hesitates.

The only sound comes from the Appaloosa shaking the rain off his back.

There is no way Hart is going to fold, on his home

territory, in front of all these witnesses, to a girl.

He sees the bet, though his hands are shaking.

'What have you got?' he snarls.

'You first.'

He reveals the seven and four of diamonds. With the river it is a flush. Pretty strong.

When Kelly makes no move, I fear the worst and Hart leers at her. 'Come on, sweetheart. I know you been bluffin' on scraps.'

Kelly peels her concealed cards over one at a time, to an eerie gasp from the audience. Queen of clubs and the ten of hearts. With the river, that makes three queens and a pair of tens. She has a full house.

Luis whistles in relief. Me – I'm thinking about landing one on her anyway.

Kelly winks at Hart and rakes in the pot. Hart looks fit to explode, but then an unsavoury looking character stoops to whisper in his ear.

'Hold up now, Miss Tillman. I declare that game void.'

'On what grounds?'

'That there horse is stolen property. Weren't yours to sell in the first place.'

'Oh, put a cork in it, Hart!' pipes up Josie. 'The girl won fair and square.'

Hart's voice is sly and wheedling. 'Ain't worth nothing to you if that horse belongs to someone else. Why don't you check up by its mane?'

I glance over at Luis for ideas. He gives me the slightest shake of his head and looks around for exits. But a crowd is closing in. This is an ugly situation about to turn uglier.

Josie turns up the Appaloosa's mane and there's another collective round of murmuring. 'Hey, what you trying to pull here?'

'What's the problem?' I ask, knowing full well what the problem is, but I'm hoping Kelly will catch my drift. The only way out of this is to leave the winnings on the table as we leave.

Josie pulls one of her enormous blunderbusses. 'The problem, little lady, is that this horse got scorpion branding. It's an outlaw ride – Jethro Boys. It ain't worth two eighty-five. Hell, it ain't worth glue.'

I wonder then if she has so much as an inkling that the Jethro Gang consists of Visitors.

'We'll give you back what you paid for it,' I offer.

'And ten dollars more,' adds Luis.

'After she tried to palm me off with a horse I couldn't give away?' she scoffs. 'You're gonna be doing a might better than that.'

'The game's void,' repeats Hart, as Kelly begins to stuff the winnings into her jeans pockets.

'Er . . . I guess that means you're under arrest,' says the man I take to be the Sheriff of Brokeoff. He has a timid demeanour, and I suspect he has survived into old age by being both a coward and a turner of blind eyes.

'On what charge, goddamn it?' cries Kelly.

'Possession of stolen property, fraud, being part of a criminal outfit, underage gambling,' says Hart with a triumphant smile. 'Take your pick. Now, the game is void.' He stands quickly, with his hands hovering over the holsters. 'So, I suggest you give up the pot so these gentlemen can take back their wagers.'

'Not before I get my two eighty-five,' warns Josie. 'And then some.' She levels the gun at Kelly's head.

'Now, now, Josie. I'm the one making arrests round here,' complains the sheriff.

'If you wanna continue your custom here, Sheriff, then you'd best butt on out of this one.' She pulls back the hammer on the blunderbuss.

Nobody moves.

And then in the silence, another gun is cocked.

'I believe I can bring this tricky matter to a close,' a voice announces.

The intruder is possibly the ugliest man I have ever seen. The bush of nasal hair sprouting from each nostril of his pig nose looks something like a moustache. His eyes are tiny dead dots. He has only one hand in which he brandishes a pistol. The sleeve of his left arm is pinned to his shirt to stop it flapping about.

Josie doesn't lower her blunderbuss. 'And who the hell are you?'

'My name is Virgil Bridgwater, and I have a bill of sale for that horse.'

A BARGAIN WITH
THE DEVIL

The name of my father leaves me stunned. I do not listen to the bluster and swearing of Hart who has gone from loser to winner to loser in the space of five minutes. I have my attention only on this stranger, this *imposter*.

'Well then, Mr Bridgwater, let's see your bill of sale,' says Josie, retaining both her poise and her grip on the blunderbuss.

'There's a rip under the saddle – it's in there. For three

hundred and five dollars.'

The toad who informed Hart about the scorpion marks by the mane duly checks and produces a yellowing and much folded document. 'As the man says.'

I catch Kelly's eye – an incredulous look that says, *That's your dad?*

And I want to yell out to the entire saloon that he is not. But of course at this moment he remains our best hope of walking from this place scot-free. It does not take a genius to realise he is at least an accessory to the theft of my father's horse, which makes him a probable outlaw of the Jethro Gang. And therefore in all likelihood a Visitor.

'So to recap here,' says the stranger, holstering his gun expertly. 'If that horse belongs to me, it ain't stolen. And if it ain't stolen, the game stands. And if the game stands, the winnings got won above board. Stands to reason the sale to the landlady was lee-git also. Now we can sit here and write out a new bill of sale, Ma'am, except I figure you don't wanna explain away them scorpions when you come to sell him on. So why don't I buy the horse back at your first asking price? That way you walk away with the fastest profit you ever made in this here sa-loon.'

His accent and manner are so convincing, it is hard to believe he is Visitor, not human. Certainly, the saloon regulars are fooled.

'And who's to say you really are this Mr Bridgwater?' demands Hart. A good question.

'Well, my wayward and unruly children, Sir. Who else?' He beams an insufferably smug smile, daring me to contradict him.

I say nothing. Luis takes a breath to say something but I warn him off with a sharp look. Denying the stranger's story will only complicate matters right now, especially given how edgy the saloon has become.

The pretend Mr Bridgwater addresses the crowd. 'Allow me to apologise – the fault is all mine. But who are we to indulge if not our offspring?'

I only gaze at this smarmy act unfolding before me as if it were a cheap travelling sideshow. The salesman laying down his patter. My rage is cold. But I must not puncture this lie. Our fate depends upon it. And of course, this imposter must know something of my father.

'You sure took your time,' announces Kelly, even frowning herself at the outrageous breezy tone she has adopted. '*Daddy*.'

It is stretching credulity indeed to believe that this fine blonde girl and that shifty specimen are blood. But he presents a way out of a tricky impasse – one that Josie grasps. She puts away her gun and smiles which thaws the atmosphere in the room. Everyone plays their part in the charade that follows – money changes hands, backs are slapped, drinks are bought for the card game losers. The sheriff is cowed. Any notion I entertained of appealing to justice is quickly dispelled as he lines up for his own shot of the cloudy moonshine.

Kelly, Luis and I retreat through the rain to the stables with the imposter. He brings the Appaloosa, and it is strange how he doesn't bother with the reins – just touches the neck near the mane. The horse walks with him calmly, as if he is indeed the true owner. Only when we're outside do I realise his fingers are resting on the hidden scorpion brand.

Right by the barn door, Luis swivels and reaches for the stranger's holster. But it's a wild move – Luis is parried and thrown against the doorpost with explosive force. From the floor, Luis gathers himself to attack again, but the stranger draws his gun so fast it's cocked and pointing before any of us moves.

'Don't be getting any fancy ideas,' he mutters. 'I'll put a bullet through the next one of you that tries something.'

His eyes suddenly blaze at us – peepholes to the fires behind the mask, leaving no doubt that he is Visitor. He . . . It . . . .? I cannot reconcile the creature before me. It seems impossible that nothing remains of the man but flesh. *Is there not some vestige of humanity there in that vessel of blood and bone? Something we can appeal to?* He does not appear at all handicapped by being one-armed – he controls the three of us with ease, taking possession of all our guns before mounting his own horse. He ropes a mule laden with supplies to the pommel of his saddle and gestures for us to mount up. Luis and I climb on Cisco, Kelly gets back on the Appaloosa that once belonged to Pa.

Hodges watches us from under the dripping eaves. There is no more understanding in him than what goes on between the ears of a horse. For a wild moment I think of conversing with him to see if, as Josie warned, he will flare up in temper. Perhaps in the confusion we might escape, though it seems unlikely we will get far.

The townsfolk must be sheltering from the rain

because the main drag is empty. Once we're out of the town, the Visitor orders me to tie Luis's hands behind his back for good measure. We ride slowly north towards the mountains, single file, the Visitor on his horse bringing up the rear, trailing the pack-mule.

'Who are you?' I demand over my shoulder.

The Visitor doesn't answer. For twenty minutes we ride through the rain, across Route 62 into the foothills of the Guadalupe Mountains.

Luis whispers in my ear, 'Ride, Megan!'

'Are you crazy?' I hiss back.

'He doesn't shoot. They want you alive, no?'

'That won't stop him shooting *you* in the back. Besides, what about Kelly?'

'She has her horse. We meet in Canyon de Chelly if we split.'

'Forget it. It's not her horse – it belongs to the Visitors now it has the scorpion mark. That's how he tracked us down. Besides, Kelly can't navigate through the Zone on her own. It's suicide.'

The Visitor rides abreast of us. 'Quit yabbering!'

He stays within earshot but it gives me a chance to observe him and after a while I recognise something. He is maintaining a perimeter, as trackers do. My thoughts race in confusion and surprise. It is not what I expected – that Visitors should ever need to be wary in the Zone they have themselves created.

'Where's my father? What have you done with him?'

'Your father is as good as dead, honey,' he says out of the corner of his mouth. 'No escape for him.'

I search the Visitor's face for clues but he is impassive. What reason would he have to lie? So, then my father *is* alive and captured. So if the messages are from him, how is he able to send them? In secret? Or perhaps he is being coerced and the messages are a trick to draw me deeper into the Zone?

Kelly turns in her saddle. 'Sure was going outta your way to blend in back there in town. Guess you ain't so strong on your lonesome, huh? Without the rest of Jethro's gang. They'da lynched you in that saloon if they got wind of what you really are.'

'Wanna know how come I lasted so long in wretched towns like that up and down the Zone?' he drawls for effect and turns his collar up against the rain – such a natural gesture. 'I watch your kind real close. And I kill any human that "*gets wind of what I really am*".' The Visitor bares his teeth at Kelly – more of a warning than a smile. 'Reckon I'm gonna let you live for a while. Two females'll give me all the cover I need to *blend in* 'til we reach White Sands. But the wetback here – he ain't gonna be so lucky.'

He pulls up his horse and flicks his gun at me. 'Come on, child. You know the score. There's a shovel in my pack. Get busy with it now.' His voice is utterly callous. Only now do I see the hopelessness of reasoning with him. We have been led as lambs to the slaughter.

'You can't,' I stammer.

'I can and I will.'

'You're gonna shoot him,' Kelly says flatly. It's as if she has just realised that this is not a game.

'Yep. When there's a big enough hole to put him in. This seems a good a spot as any.'

Luis says nothing, just glares at the Visitor in defiance.

'Spare him,' I say when I can be sure my voice will hold steady.

'He's one surly son of a gun and he's been itching to land one on me since I bailed you out that sa-loon. I ain't riding a hundred miles to the rendezvous watching my back every step of the way.'

'Then let him go.'

'So he's free to sneak up on us ten miles from now?'

I get ready to beg, though I know it will do no good. The cruelty of the Visitor knows no bounds and, worse than that, it is casual, everyday. There is a pitiless logic to it – the grave is only to hide Luis's body from the prying eyes of Brokeoff's citizens.

Luis takes aim and spits at the Visitor's face. He speaks in Spanish, to me, knowing the game is up.

'I am ready before God. I go to my family. Is for you to win, Megan.' These are last words and I cannot bear to hear them. My heart is already broken as I start to plead with the Visitor.

'Nope. He's a dead dog and if you ain't digging then he can die now.' He cocks his gun.

'No! Wait!' Kelly cries. She jumps from her horse. 'I'll dig.'

I stare at her, insensible, undone.

The Visitor nods, pleased that his control of the situation is complete.

Luis says to Kelly. '*Cavar lento*,' breathes Luis. *Dig slow*.

She answers him in Spanish. 'I've won prizes for my slow digging.'

'Our friend is not so good at blending in with Mexicans then,' says Luis.

The Visitor doesn't react. So he doesn't understand Spanish or he doesn't care.

I stare at my companions in stunned silence. They have won a reprieve I could not have won – a bargain with the devil. Another few breaths of life in return for digging a grave. And while there's life there is still a chance. I quieten my terror and feel out into the Zone around me – a silent prayer of sorts. But the Zone does not answer. It is aloof from human concerns.

'Hey, wake up, Zone-girl,' says Kelly to me in Spanish. 'I need distractions. And it'd be real handy to know weak spots on these critters.'

'Enough talk,' barks the Visitor.

Kelly yanks the shovel free from its straps. She throws me a wide-eyed look, then she thrusts the shovel into the mud with grim gusto.

'So, White Sands,' she says, like we're talking about a vacation. 'What happens there?'

I think she is mad, baiting the Visitor like this. But then he answers, in a distracted manner, bitter and bored. Almost as if he is talking to himself. 'Gotta get the right side of them land rivers before they get up a head of speed, else you can't make north more than Flagstaff.'

Kelly throws me a questioning look perhaps in reference to *land rivers*. But I have no idea what they are.

Distractions. Any throw of the dice is worth it now.

'My father knows I'm coming,' I try. 'He sends me messages.'

The Visitor shakes his head.

'You don't believe me? I've got a map in my pack that leads to Canyon de Chelly. Navajo Nation.'

With one eye on us, the Visitor rifles through my expedition pack on Cisco. He pulls out my Rand McNally atlas and the hand-drawn map flutters free.

'This where you're headed? Mavis Pilgrim mail route?' He thrusts the map at me. 'And them graves? What's the cemetery?'

Over his shoulder, Kelly inches closer, all the while keeping a steady rhythm with her digging.

'Spider Rock. There's a grave I must find.'

'Whose grave?'

I squint at him through the rain, floundering for something, anything that will keep this conversation going. He doesn't know about the cemetery, he doesn't know about the grave.

'My mother,' I blurt at last.

Kelly winces like I've said the wrong thing.

But the Visitor's reaction is remarkable. 'Your mother! That witch! We should have hunted her down sooner.'

'What did she ever do to you?' I cry. The misery of her death rises in me – I was too young to know her.

A dreadful expression passes over the Visitor's stolen face – a kind of gloating disgust.

'You don't know, do you?' he says at last.

My heart begins to hammer.

'Know what?'

'*La cabeza*, Kelly,' says Luis. The head.

And that's when Kelly lands the back of the shovel full force into the side of the Visitor's skull.

AS THREE

For a moment we all just look at the Visitor lying awkwardly in the mud.

'Had it pegged from the get-go,' says Kelly. 'Might be from outer space but I can spot the type. Used to get them coming in the Taco-Shack-O all day long. Long-distance truckers fixing to shoot their mouth off.'

This deadpan claim so astounds me that I can find no reply. I untie Luis in a daze.

Kelly prods the Visitor with her boot. 'Reckon it's dead?'

As soon as he's free, Luis snatches up the loose

handgun from the dirt. 'Dead? Not yet. The sheriff, he say between the eyes.'

'No! Luis, no!' I cry.

Kelly pulls him back. 'Whoa there, cowboy. Not 'til it's told me what I wanna know. That thing's gonna spill it all – Valentine, abduction, who's dead, who's alive. Every damn detail. Then we can both finish the job.'

'No one's going to do any killing!'

'What the hell do you care, you lame-ass? They popped your aunt. They're sure as hell gonna pop you soon as they get what they want.'

I think about the Visitor at the sheriff's office in Marfa – how I could not murder it even when it pushed me to do so. Why? I feel no qualms – it is more like a line I cannot cross.

'We have to learn from the Zone to defend ourselves. Pa said killing in cold blood wasn't the way,' I manage, struggling to keep some authority in my voice.

Kelly is genuinely amazed. 'It ain't got any blood like ours, Megan. Except what it's stolen. It's a parasite!'

'What do you know about it?' I challenge. '*I've* told you everything you know about Visitors.'

'Even that!' she splutters, working up her rage. 'The way you call 'em Visitors. Like they're just coming over for a chilli cook-out. Like frickin' neighbours! They ain't visitors, they're invaders. Meat-eatin' hunters. And they're here to stay!'

'You will gain nothing by killing this creature.'

'This is war!' she shouts at me. 'Lock'n'load. It's the enemy! Give me one good reason why I shouldn't blow it straight to hell right now.'

She strides over to the Visitor's horse and pulls free the shotgun. 'They're all dead anyhow, right? My folks. Everyone I know in that town. Give me one good reason.'

She has stoked herself into a fury of fear and hate, on the edge of tears. She lines the shotgun barrels up with the Visitor's head and closes one eye.

My thinking right then is cold and it is clear. I remember the sudden rage that rose in me at the saloon at Kelly's rash behaviour – that inescapable urge for violence. In Kelly now, that urge must be countless times stronger, where murder is the only release. I never felt like that even when Pa disappeared, even when my aunt was gunned down.

'I'll give you three reasons,' I say quietly.

Luis hangs his head, drops his handgun back onto the ground. But Kelly moves her aim closer, as if that will harden her resolve.

'You are in the Zone,' I say. 'And the Zone judges you.'

'Bull crap.'

'What you do here, your deeds and the outcome of your deeds, are part of the Zone. That is how it works in this place. An unnecessary stray shot alerts our presence to others. You cannot predict the consequences of a reckless act.'

Even as I say this, my mind hovers over a truth that remains just out of reach. Something about the Visitor lying there defenceless. Something about the Zone, about what it really is . . .

The shotgun shakes in Kelly's hands.

'They *are* the enemy,' I say. 'But slaughtering this one Visitor will not help to defeat them. They turned the moon into dust. They stopped this world on its axis. They take our flesh at will. We cannot match them in a straight conflict. We have to understand them if we are to save ourselves.'

'Swear to God almighty, reason number three gotta be better than one and two.'

And then it comes to me. It is a revelation that I feel sure my father must have uncovered because he did not try like others to raise an army. *He went into the Zone . . .* The Zone is something the Visitors have created, or unleashed. It has a *purpose*. It was not here before they came. And yet. They do not control it. This Visitor maintained a perimeter as trackers do. He was mindful of it, as if it holds just as much peril for them as for us. He seeks to reach White Sands because that is where Zone travellers may cross *land rivers before they get a head of steam*. They cannot traverse this country any more easily than we can.

Kelly gives me a wild look, daring me to stop her.

Luis steps forward and holds his hand out for the shotgun.

'What? You goin' soft on me? What about your family, Luis? What about them?'

His face darkens in anger but he does not reply.

'If you pull that trigger, Kelly, we're through,' I tell her. 'You're on your own. That a good enough reason for you?'

She gulps at her breaths, scrapes away her tears.

'Goddamn Miss High'n'Mighty! Ain't gonna be a soul to miss this sonofabitch!'

'That's true. But just think about afterwards, Kelly.'

'Shut your mouth!'

I think about how she won't be the same Kelly Tillman if she shoots this defenceless Visitor. None of us will be the same. I look at Luis and he is staring at me, more miserable than I have ever seen him. He has given up on her already – he whispers something in Spanish quickly. A prayer I think. For the words are rote. A prayer not for the Visitor, but for us. We will unravel if she shoots. He senses it as well as I. We will not survive the Zone apart. But as three we are strong. I see it so clearly, but I cannot force her – she must see it on her own, or not at all. If she would only look up at us, it would save her. In that moment, I can think of nothing else. I want us to be just as we were. Before Brokeoff.

She steadies her aim. I really think she's going to do it – all her frustration rising to a peak . . .

She pulls the gun to one side and fires. One, two, three rounds into the mud.

The noise stirs the Visitor from his groggy state. He looks then in abject fear at Kelly – is it real, this emotion? Or mimicked to save his life?

Kelly flings the gun into the grass, drops to her knees and delivers her hardest punch into the Visitor's face. He slumps back with a grunt.

She shakes out her fingers. 'Well, what we gonna do with it? We can't just leave it here.'

I'm so relieved I want to embrace her. But she does not meet our gaze, somehow furious with herself or with us – I cannot say.

It is Luis who moves first. He takes rope from Cisco and ties the Visitor's arms and legs together as though hobbling a steer. Then he tosses the captive's boots into the scrub so the spurs cannot be used to wear down the rope. Finally, he gags him with a neckerchief. I cannot imagine what Luis is thinking as he does this – by all rights he should be dead. By now, the Visitor is conscious again, straining every sinew, eyes popping.

'Good as dead anyhow if you leave it like that,' mutters Kelly.

For an uncomfortable length of time we stare at his pathetic form rolling about like a trussed turkey.

Finally, Luis unropes the Visitor's pack-mule and leads it down the hill a way.

'Hey, what you doing?' cries Kelly.

Luis slaps its rump hard and whoops at it to be gone. It charges away back towards town.

'Great. You wanna check in with us before you do stuff?' yells Kelly.

Luis glares at her. 'Like you. At this saloon. You gamble with our lives, Kelly.'

'They see a loaded-up mule in that town, they're gonna send out a search party!' She points at the captive. 'You want it coming back on our trail? Now I'm gonna have to kill it all over again!'

The only sound comes from the hiss of rain and the horses sloshing about in puddles. Cisco shakes and whinnies.

'What *were* you doing in the saloon?' I ask at last. 'We were meant to be keeping a low profile.'

'What is this – the third degree? I was earning us some greenbacks, your honour. That supplies run cleaned us out case you never realised. Don't believe me, ask the Boy With No Brain over there.'

'You were selling our horse to stay in the game when I last checked.'

'So what? I knew what I was doing. That's what you do in poker – laugh at their goddamn jokes, drink their whiskey, make out you're a sap on a losing streak. I softened them up for three hours before that hand . . .'

All this is true. I have seen it happen before at the Welcome, though rarely with such style. And yet, there is more than what Kelly is telling me. I can see it in the way she turns unnecessarily on the Visitor captive.

'Will you quit rolling about?' She shoves him onto his side with her boot. 'If you must know, I landed us enough dough for another horse. And while I was at it, I found out about the Mavis Pilgrim . . .' She looks to the sky in disgust. 'Hell, I just saved our asses here! You all just forget that?'

'Megan . . .' As I turn to face Luis, he tumbles into my arms.

Over his shoulder, I see Cisco swaying and then his forelegs buckle.

Luis searches for my eyes, as though his sight is failing him. 'The Zone, Megan. The Zone . . .'

And then I feel it also. Too late. I have allowed my perimeter to lapse. I have made the unforgivable mistake of ignoring the Zone. It is upon us. A creeping slumber over the mind. Sleeping sickness. It settles, as numbing and soft as new snow. The Visitor ceases to struggle against his bindings. Kelly's anger drifts into rambling. And I fall to my knees.

SLEEPING SICKNESS

This trance has no feeling. Pieces of my mind mist over – just a mere stump of reason keeps me moving. I know we will surely die if we succumb to sleep. We will lie down insensible in the wet mud and wither from thirst or exposure. This prospect is a firebrand in my head but I feel neither fear nor sorrow. It is the Zone come to take lives, as it does every day, without passion or remorse.

Kelly is still on her feet, mumbling nonsense, weaving into the scrub like a drunk. I call to her but she hears nothing.

The Visitor who brought us here lies corpse-like, his

empty sleeve unpinned and trailing in a puddle. I scarcely remember a thing about him.

Luis is too heavy to hold. I let him go as gently as I can, grasping for the answer to a question that now eludes me. The answer is . . . horse. The question is . . . how to escape. There will be currents, even in this sluggish veil – gradients perhaps, where a person may remain at least alert enough to move.

I drag Luis by the belt over to Cisco. My horse gives whinnies of distress as though smarting at nightmares. Blinkers of darkness draw around my eyes leaving only a tunnel of light. But once I reach Cisco's flanks, gleaming in the rain, I feel a little stronger, and he too launches himself upright. It is as though we give succour through touch, one to the other. It takes all my strength just to hoist Luis over the front of the saddle. I stand there for what could be hours for all I know, gathering up my wits and losing them again.

God only knows how long it takes me to mount Cisco and corral the other horses. I use rope, fumbling with it like a child, pulling the creatures into a gaggle around me. I have to call out my purpose over and over in a mantra to keep focused, and several times I look at the hopeless loops in my hands and wonder what I'm doing. I dare not dismount – the dumb breathing of the animals is all that lies between the sleep and me.

I try to maintain my perimeter, staring down a closing tunnel of blindness. The sleep comes in waves, sweeping down from the mountains, I think, like the ghost of a glacier. At last I find Kelly, more by luck than judgment.

She is swaying with her arms outstretched, oaths spilling from her lips, drowning slowly – just anger sustaining her now.

I cannot afford to tussle, so I rope her with a lariat, take the strain onto the pommel of my saddle so the line pulls tight around her shoulders and draw her stumbling from the slopes. It takes all my concentration to ride through rough country with Luis on board and lead the other horses, not to mention Kelly. Instinct takes me back towards the highway and for a brief spell my head clears. I need to turn west to skirt the southern spur of the Guadalupe Mountains, then head north towards the Lincoln Forest – this is the most sensible route towards Canyon de Chelly. But I haven't walked Cisco more than a hundred metres towards the sun before a great front of sleep lies down over me. It nearly unseats me, and in a panic so maddening and clumsy, I u-turn – east along the 180, just exactly where I don't want to go. But it's as if the Zone, becalmed for so long, is now goading us along a corridor with invisible currents.

Poor Kelly has keeled over and is being dragged through the mire at the side of the road. I'm too plain scared to stop now in case the sleep overtakes me. I wonder at how I have resisted it at all, given the state of my companions. Perhaps the rest I took at the Drunken Steer is now paying dividends. Or my Zone sense has saved me. I cannot tell. The horses stumble, their heads stooped. Slumber presses overhead and to the sides of my passage, tipping me into horrible jerky naps. I bite my tongue and pinch myself blue. Thoughts run away even as

I force my eyes wide open. Thank the Lord for the rain at least. I take off my hat and let it course cold down my collar. I tie myself to the pommel in a tangle of knots that would make a cowboy laugh but perhaps it will keep me from falling.

The grasses all about are beaten down by the rain, heads heavier than stalks. For a terrifying mile I am unable to summon a reliable likeness of my pa. But then in a moment of absurd triumph I conjure his face. It is just a snapshot, pre-Visitation, before I was born. It is one that I treasure, somewhere in my expedition pack. He is caught in laughter, in rude health, facing someone off-camera, sharing a joke that must remain forever hidden now. His head thrown back to the impossible blue glare of a Texas sky.

It is his carefree ways that I miss above all else – how he would on a whim take me into the off-Zone country-side and show me what he knew about nature, beetles and toads and birds. Just the adventure of the outside. For days and nights under the sky. With him alone it was easy somehow to be just me. No one else could ever make me feel like that – happy in my own skin. These dreams and visions I've had in the Zone – if they come from anyone, they *must* come from him! I imagine them cast from his spirit, these messages, travelling through rock and tree and air, through the fabric of the Zone. But do they come to me from a living man, or a ghost?

Awake! Focus.

Somewhere along that road, with steep shoulders of rock to my left and barren scrub to my right, I realise with an awful jolt where I am being driven. It is a place laid down in almanacs of Zone tracking. It is marked on my Rand McNally in red ink. No-go. One of the great static danger areas of the Zone that must be avoided at all costs. Carlsbad. I have paid it no attention, for our course was set to go nowhere near it, but the rolling banks of sleep either side give me no choice.

As a test I coax Cisco southward – perhaps I can find a route clear in the desert. But even a few metres shy of the line I feel the onset of coma. I am hemmed in. Maybe the roaming sleep is a feature of Carlsbad – an outlying satellite of its main peril, snagging unsuspecting travellers to their deaths. For it seems too coincidental that these forces are tugging us to a place that Zone trackers would sell their souls to avoid.

For miles and miles I fight sleep. Strangely, it is the dread of Carlsbad that keeps me awake. There are no accounts of the dangers there. None have returned to tell the tale. Pre-Visitation it was a haunt of tourists drawn to the caverns, home to a colony of ten million bats. But now? The Zone is a consummate keeper of secrets.

If I could get Cisco into a canter I might break free, but he is locked at crawling pace, and anyway I have Kelly to think about bumping across the country like a hay bale. But any hopes I have of outrunning the situation are dashed when I spot a family of javelina pigs charging from cover ahead. They squeal and scatter but they are taken by the sleep, ploughing their snouts into the mud just a stone's throw from me. I am in a moving bubble but I must stay within it to survive.

The path of that bubble brings me first away from, then back to the mountains. We veer sharply from the highway and into a pass, beyond the crumbling structures of White's City – an old stopping point before the caverns. Here lie the ruins of an America long gone – motels and gift shops and fake wigwams and concrete posts that previously bore neon and blaring signs. It is the America Kelly once knew, where she took uneventful family vacations. Indian lands overrun by white men and overrun yet again by Visitors.

I check the rifle and my revolver are both loaded and try to wake Luis again and again, but he will not be roused.

Up a winding valley road. Clouds stream over the summits of rock. The rain peters out and there against a grey sky I see the first spiral of bats – a great black funnel, like slow-motion smoke. The exodus is mesmerising – twisting and eddying through the air in nervous shoals. I come to a kind of open-air amphitheatre cut into the rock. Above me the bats are a whisper of papery wings. Scattered amongst the steps are skeletons – horse and human, some more recent than others.

The sleep evaporates as I reach the lip of the cavern. Luis stirs and behind me I hear Kelly cry out.

'What's going on?' mumbles Luis.

'Trouble.'

Cisco pulls up, sniffing the air warily.

Sharp tang of ammonia and smoke and boiled meat.

There are scruffy vegetable patches clinging to the soils around me.

I do not like this place.

For a while, I cannot make much out in the shadows of the overhang – it is too gloomy. But then I notice that there are people waiting there. They stare at us, not offering any kind of greeting. Their grimy faces are half-starved and sullen. The men lean on rakes, not moving except to brush away the flies. The women peer from the openings of a few threadbare tents. The children have bow legs and the pot-bellies of famine. Some are naked to the cold.

I should feel fear and I do, but it hovers only on the surface of my mind, not deep where it can rule me. Is it fear or just the semblance of fear, like the emotions Visitors conjure to seem human? I make sure these inhabitants can see my rifle, but I already know that to be armed in this place will do no good. It is a sinkhole in the Zone, surrounded by the sleep. These people are marooned here and their savage faces tell me there is no escape. We are just the latest castaways and if we are to survive we must live by their rules.

A man with the bloodied lips and black teeth of scurvy finds the strength to hail us.

'Well, looky here. What the tide's washed up. The Zone provideth, the Zone taketh away.'

It is the way the man does not look at me, only at the shifting trio of horses, that makes my mind up. I stuff my revolver for safekeeping into one of Cisco's saddlebags. I dismount slowly with Luis and wait for Kelly to free herself of the lariat, then I raise the rifle and fire it. My screams drive the horses into a commotion and when one bolts, they all bolt, roped together into a chaotic blunder across the amphitheatre. They make it as far as a spillage of boulders up on the old road, slowing and knocking into each other before collapsing. Their breathing calms as the sleep takes them.

I fling the rifle as far as I can into the weeds where it cannot be fired again.

The camp is in shock.

Kelly swears under her breath. 'Megan, tell me you ain't mad. Tell me you didn't lose it out there.'

'You see any horses in this place?' I demand, willing her to understand. 'They have no need of them.'

'But they're gonna die up there.'

'Rather that than be butchered and eaten here. Anyhow they're *not* going to die.' But even as I say the words I wonder whether I really believe them.

As one, the people of this cavern edge closer. Their eyes burn with hunger and fury.

It is Luis that surely saves us from a lynching. He springs onto a rock ledge at the mouth of the cavern and to the astonishment of everyone gathered, takes his dagger and slashes a cross in blood across his chest.

His appeal to them is fervent and real. It could only have been delivered in his native Spanish for his English is too halting and spare. I have never heard him speak this way. It is both a plea and a warning.

'Listen to me,' he tells them. 'We have been sent for a reason, to deliver you from this place. A great storm of Zone forces has driven us at God's beckoning to this haven of bats. We have braved much danger and tribula-

146

tion to be here. To harm us would be to violate God's purpose.'

Those who understand Spanish murmur translations to their companions.

Someone cries, 'Ain't no God's purpose round about here.'

Luis continues almost in a fever, eyes wide, plucking words from I know not where. He explains that it is true that God's will finds no sanctuary here, in this forsaken trap of the Zone, but this is why we have come.

'The bats here travel as much as twenty miles in a night, feeding on the fly. Before Visitation they would consume a vast weight of insects contaminated with pesticide poison that did them no immediate harm but remained deposited in their bodies like a chemical time bomb. Only once they began their long migration to caves in Mexico for the winter would the pesticide they had consumed take its toll. For as they flew south the weakest ones used up their reserves of fat, releasing the poison at last into their blood. And when it reached their brains they would drop out of the sky to their deaths.'

Luis looks at them, stalling for breath or inspiration, judging the mood of his audience. They are attentive but grow impatient for the point.

'Come on, keep on going,' whispers Kelly.

He tells them if men feed upon evil, it will store in their hearts and when they are tested it will spread into their bloodstreams and kill them.

'You people are trapped here by the world that has stopped turning,' he cries in Biblical Spanish. 'You are being challenged by God. Through the Zone, He watches, to see if your hearts are filled with poison. But if you spare us, you will see your reward on Earth and in Heaven.'

The blood blooms across his shirt.

As they stare at us I cannot tell what they will do. It is as though they are waiting for a further sign. But Luis is spent.

The only sound comes from the corkscrew of bats overhead – a chatter of beating wings.

The man who hailed us speaks up then. 'Well, seems we is *blessed* by these here *outsiders*. What we gone done with our manners, huh? Come now, you must be weary from all your travellin'. I'm Wesley Carmichael and I'm what makes for a chief round here.'

He offers a damp hand and appraises every part of me except for my eyes. It is as though he is assessing my strength or the meat on my bones.

No one in the community moves.

'Come now,' growls Wesley Carmichael. 'Let's be offering these folks some of that famous Carlsbad *hospitality*!'

He leads us down a path beneath a sharp overhang.

'Where'd all that fire and brimstone come from?' Kelly mutters to Luis.

Luis looks dazed. A sideways glance at me. 'Chapel in Marfa. The father . . . he preach this story of bats.'

I, too, have been there for Sunday services when my aunt insisted. It is something all townsfolk are expected to do, but religion has made little impression on me. However, Luis, it seems, has absorbed these sermons – his performance just now could not have succeeded otherwise. It makes me realise – I do not know him as well as I'd imagined.

Wesley leads us towards a cauldron set upon a fire of dung bricks. A tiny crone picks up a net of black shapes and smacks it against the cave wall. It's not until I get closer through the fumes and steam that I see the stunned bodies of bats in the netting – their pug faces like a hoard of miniature demons.

She stares at me through her cataracts and guts the bats one by one with a practised swipe of her cleaver, then tosses them into the pot.

'Great,' mumbles Kelly. 'Bat stew cooked on a bat shit fire by an old bat.'

I nudge her in the ribs, because I feel sure that Kelly's humour will not be appreciated in this place.

'Thanks all the same,' says Kelly aiming an injured glare at me. 'But I just ate at the last town.'

'Might as well get used to it, sugar,' snaps the crone. 'Bats is all we got. Exceptin' turnips. And they done shot with maggots this year.'

GUANO MINES

Kelly refuses but I don't know where the next meal is coming from so I tuck in. The broth is salty and littered with lumps of contorted leather that I do not examine closely.

Wesley Carmichael talks to us in a way that manages to be both friendly and menacing. His hand is never far from a machete he keeps tucked in his belt and there are two sullen and watchful men who hover nearby. They look better fed than the other inhabitants of Carlsbad – one is armed with an ice-pick, the other has a club bristling with nails. It is clear to me that we have earned some kind of reprieve but dissent is not an option.

After the meal, Carmichael splits us up. Kelly is carted off to help till the vegetable plots and mend bat nets, whilst Luis and I are given a shift in the guano mines. Perhaps it is a punishment for our indiscretions – me for scaring the horses to safety, Luis for stealing his chiefly thunder.

At the end of a path, deep in the cavern shadow, we are shown to a rusty bucket on a chain dangling over a drop into nothingness. Wesley hands us shovels and a lantern with a candle.

The bucket is just big enough for Luis and I to squeeze into. We hold hands as we tip into the gloom, chain creaking over the toothed wheels of an old winch. The lantern flame whips a weak light across the walls. The bat exodus is almost over but out of the depths come a few stragglers, wheeling up in panic.

By the time we are at the bottom, the cavern opening is just a coin of dim light far above. Between us we drag the bucket down a slippery path. It is an eerie place of cave pillars and dripping rock curtains. From the walls hooded phantoms and death heads appear to us in the stuttering candle flame. We crunch over dead bats – the young who have fallen from their roosts. At last we come to the guano pits – layers of compacted sludge that clog the spaces between stalagmites. A reek lies over the cave floor like a poisonous mist, stinging my eyes so badly I have to dig blind for the most part.

At one point I look up into the darkness and pain snatches my head. A silent semaphore of sickly light. A message? I fight for balance in the gloom. This forsaken hole . . . we are here for a reason. I see glimpses of hatchling creatures, millions of them, like the bats of Carlsbad, roosting in the crevices of a place, not here, but far away, deep in the Zone. They bide their time, growing in the dark. A nest of the Visitors before they take human bodies?

'Megan?'

'Hush a minute!'

Carlsbad, this cave, it is special. Why? My senses race through the shadows for an answer. It is like a miniature Zone! A zone within a zone. People are trapped in Carlsbad, stranded because they don't understand this place, how they might escape it. But its secret is here, at the heart, and if I look hard enough I will know it!

A smell surrounds me – one that I know so well. Warm, tobacco, old leather. 'Pa?'

The smell is swamped by the reek of guano. The flashes of light vanish. The pain dissipates.

'Megan?' Luis takes my hand.

I cling to the residue of the message – what does it mean? Secrets unveiled in the darkness? Look for clues in your surroundings? Perhaps this place is a test – a way to learn mastery of the Zone.

My breathing steadies. 'It is nothing. I am just tired.'

It occurs to me then. Why have I not shared these messages with my companions? Why don't I want to share them with Luis now? It is not lack of trust, I decide. I think on it alone. Our journey is shared, but these messages are from Pa and they are just for me. The words of the Visitor return: *You don't know, do you?* There is something I must confront. And I must confront it alone.

An hour later, we've hoisted the bucket on its hook and there is a brief chance to get our breath back as the payload is hauled up. Luis wipes my eyes gently with a handkerchief he has somehow managed to keep clean. I inspect the wounds he inflicted on his chest – they are not deep but I am worried about infection in this filthy place.

I speak to him in Spanish, as I sometimes do when we are alone. 'We must understand the Zone here if we are to escape.'

'Megan, these people have been trapped here for years, perhaps since Visitation. You saw the edges of the vegetable plots – they do not even consider venturing beyond them any more.'

'This is why they are still here – they have given up trying. They are like animals caged so long they cannot imagine freedom.'

'There are no Zone tales of Carlsbad – no one has ever returned . . .'

'There will be a way,' I insist. 'If this is a no-go area, someone must have designated it that way – a tracker who discovered its secrets.'

He hangs his head. 'I should not have given these people hope. They will turn on us if we cannot deliver them.'

'Don't be ridiculous – you bought us time. It was a brave thing to do. Have faith.' I smile at him.

He pulls a lump of guano from my hair and grins. 'Do

you think Kelly would like it down here?'

'How long was she clean for after the fish storm? A few hours? They've probably got her shaping guano patties.'

Luis's laughter echoes through unnumbered tunnels. It gives me a strange warmth, to know that I have made him laugh, in this dismal predicament. But then, as his voice carries away, I realise why they have split us up – so that we will not be tempted to search these dark tombs for a way out. Kelly is being held to ransom. I wonder how desperate we would have to become that chasing into the cavern presents itself as an attractive option. Perhaps we will know after a week, a month, a year.

It is a thought that maybe Luis shares, because he takes my hand then. 'Megan, I must tell you something,' he says solemnly. 'I meant to say at the inn.'

He swallows. I tell him that he need not say, for I am suddenly afraid. Sadness enters his eyes. *What could be so terrible?*

'I have been . . . angry. Inside. Since my family . . .'

'I know . . .'

He shakes his head. 'No, you do not know. I have sworn vengeance.'

I think of him hiding from the killers as they gun down his family. But I do not see how his confession concerns me.

'The ones I seek,' he says, waiting for me to understand. 'They are in the Zone, they are *of* the Zone. *Visitors.*'

'I know this.'

'I have no craft, no feeling for the Zone. Except what I

154

have learned from you.'

And then the dime drops. These past years he has been my friend, from the first day that I met him in the share-crop plots around my home, he has been waiting for me to lead him into the Zone. Not to help me search for my father. Not to keep me safe. Not because he likes me. But because he wishes vengeance. I think of my hopes – unrealistic perhaps – that there is a way for us all to overcome the threat of Visitation, that my father somehow holds the key to life. But it is clear now Luis has never shared that hope – perhaps he does not even expect to live once vengeance has been served.

'I have been your passage to the Zone,' I say at last. 'That is all.'

The message of this place sinks in. *Secrets unveiled in the darkness*. The hurt is actually more than I can bear, though I continue to hold his gaze in the feeble light. I am stunned, for a moment, that I could really *feel* this much. What a pitiful fool I have been. All this time, my eyes have been on these treacherous lands, dreaming of my father, picturing the moment we might be reunited. And all this time I have relied on Luis, taking his loyalty for granted. The naivety of it astounds me suddenly. It is as if I have been riding through the pages of a child's picture book – playing the heroine. I have honed my skills as a tracker and yet I am blind. Even those closest to me are a mystery.

'You planned to take your own route, once your Zone knowledge was strong enough.'

'I am sorry,' he whispers. 'It is a Zone danger when

intentions are not true, when the heart is hidden – you taught me this and I wanted to tell you many times, but I could not.'

'Why tell me now?'

'Because we will not leave this place. You must know the truth.'

I clutch his fingers and know without doubt that I would rather the truth had remained hidden.

Overhead, I hear the bucket chain rattling as it begins its descent.

I think suddenly of the sermon he has delivered to save our lives. *If men feed upon evil, it will store in their hearts and when they are tested it will spread into their bloodstreams and kill them.* His conscience must have plagued him, so that he sought solace at the chapel in Marfa. And indirectly those teachings have saved him, and us.

'You did not kill the Visitor, the one from Brokeoff,' I say at last. 'When you had the chance. You threw away the gun . . .'

He drops his head in shame. He is torn between his pledge for revenge and his disgust of it. I see it now – that his heart is more divided than ever.

'It was not among those who killed my family.'

'So, what, you're going to search the whole Zone until you find them?'

He does not answer.

I drop his hand.

I do not know where I find the strength to say it. I do not even know if it is true. 'I don't care.' *Why should he not follow his own path as I am following mine?*

'Megan . . .'

I pray that the tears in my eyes are from the fumes. Never have I cried. I saw it as weakness. But it is a freedom, like laughter. And a pain like no other. 'You are still my friend,' I manage. 'We will find a way out of this place. Then you can choose where your path lies. With me or alone.'

I turn away then, thankful for the dark. He does not break the silence. Together we work: drag, dig, fill, drag, dig, fill . . . The times we wait for the bucket are the worst. What hurts the most is that I have grown up in this dreadful hole, so suddenly, in minutes. And that my instincts of people have proven so poor.

OTHERNESS

We emerge from the mine wretched and stinking, but though it has been backbreaking work I have no thoughts of rest. I say nothing to Wesley Carmichael – the man is eager to crow over us, anticipating the breaking of our wills, and I refuse him the satisfaction. If I am to die in this filthy backwater, I will do so with my head high and my eyes clear.

Thankfully, there is a well where we can wash the worst off. The rain has stopped and there are golden breaks in the cloud, fault lines to the furnace behind. Thunder is now just a faraway warning – like the growl of a wary hound. Some Carlsbad residents offer up rags and blankets and scraps of wire for us to make a shelter. This flotsam and jetsam of garbage is no doubt a sacrifice here, where a fencing staple is precious, and I thank them, though I have no heart to build a home. I would rather sit open to the sky than give in and make roots. They stare at us – men with beards to their knees and women with stony eyes – perhaps remembering their own struggle against reality upon arrival here. Luis hunches over the shelter makings like someone absorbed in a puzzle, and I leave him then to wander through the camp.

I want to be alone with my thoughts, and to gaze out at the perimeter – fallow lands, out of reach.

The settlement is larger than I expected – spreading out along ramshackle spokes and crowded gullies, quieting down under a soft quilt of blue smoke. The boundaries are stark, butted up against wild, un-harvested brush.

Carlsbad consists of perhaps a hundred families. There is an exhausted evening calm – people murmuring by their fires and coughing. No one is strong enough to laugh or bicker.

I scout about half-heartedly for Kelly. Something tells me she is safe and adapting in her own way to the place. I find a vantage point on the weathered tilt of a boulder – somewhere she will see me when she is ready. And then I gaze down into the shadows, the snakes of mud between hovels, out to the road where Cisco lies in deadly sleep. I make out the three horses, heaped against each other – a strand of mane stirring in the breeze. At least they will be warm for now, roped together. I wonder how long they have got. Another couple of days until they will be too weak to stand anyway? I wonder if I have the strength to watch my beautiful horse rot down to bones. Perhaps if I rushed with all my heart across that ground, I would reach him in time to lie by his head before the sleep took me. The road to the first bend seems scattered with those who had the same idea, who could no longer bear Carlsbad.

But I have not the merest intention of giving in now, while there is still hope. My pa is out there somewhere in the maelstrom of forces that is the Zone. I cannot abandon him. My mind feels bright and hungry somehow. The light is restless, sunset pools that fill and shrink with the cloud tide. The Zone appears to rush by less than calling distance away. If I could just bridge that gap, I would be steeped in its currents again. This is the message from the guano mine, I know it – there are tracker clues to be gleaned from the shape of the land, or in the very nature of this predicament, if only I am sharp enough to spot them.

For some hours I probe every vista, watching for inspiration, willing an answer to present itself to me from the rocks themselves. There *will* be a way. But my workings on the problem are too haphazard, too knotted. I think the solution must be simple, staring me in the face, so clear that a child could see it. What is so frustrating, though, is the feeling that my mind already *knows* it somehow. All the pieces have been presented to me already. The bats, the cave, the patterns that repeat themselves here over and over. That is why the denizens of Carlsbad cannot see it – they have become so jaded with the view that they have abandoned hope. It is an itch I cannot pin down long enough to scratch.

Across the sky comes the first tendril of returning bats – a winding airborne river. The path darkens and swells, rippling across the skyline, but it keeps its shape – like rope. Hawks I have not noticed before launch from trees nearby. They wait until the bat river becomes a black fall into the cavern before diving into the throng with their talons, feasting on the wing. If only, I think. If only we were bats – we could just fly from here . . .

I am so engrossed in this spectacle that I don't notice Kelly. She places her palms over my eyes and bursts out laughing. This is unexpected. She's almost delirious.

'Kelly, are you all right?'

'Got something to show you!'

She drags me off the boulder and leads the way through the camp.

'What is it?'

But she will not say.

We stand at the threshold of a hollow in the rock, close to the edge of the settlement. She is breathless with excitement, but I sense something else too in her eyes – a wild, barely suppressed anxiety, that somehow this is all too good to be true.

She pulls back the tent cover.

A man looks up, eyes squinting at the light. A deep scar runs through the bridge of his nose. At first I think he is ancient, though in truth he can be no more than forty years old. An odd silence follows as Kelly fidgets, barely able to contain herself, and the man stares back, finally smiling. It is an unsure grin, as though he has not smiled for years.

Beneath the smears of dirt, the tawny matted hair, the red rims of his eyelids, he is a fine-looking fellow. He has beautiful hazel eyes. And then it hits me.

'You're Kelly's brother,' I blurt out. And immediately my mind gallops through the possibilities – has he survived Valentine like his sister? Is he a broken abductee, human but lost? Or . . .

'The very same!' cries Kelly. 'This is Lloyd. Can you believe it? What are the frickin' chances? Took me a while myself. I mean, I was digging with him a whole two hours before I cottoned on. He was just a year older than me back in Valentine, but, see, he's got older since I was on ice or whatever, so he's stretched ahead of me, ain't that right? And last time I saw him he was all fancied up for a hot date, spit-shine on his boots and a white hat like a dude.'

Kelly runs out of steam a little while I try to reconcile the heart-throb of her memory with this dishevelled man. She thumps him on the shoulder playfully, but Lloyd just stares back at me, his grin fixed.

'Well, come on then, Lloyd, don't just sit there like a prom queen! Invite us in or something. This is Megan who I just bent your ears back about for the whole day and then some. Megan, Lloyd. Lloyd, Megan.'

I gaze at his eyes, trying to see any glint of golden fire, to know if he is Visitor or human. I glance at Kelly – surely she would know? Her own flesh and blood.

I hold my hand out. Something is badly wrong here. I

think of Kelly's hysterical introduction – is she just refusing to accept the worst? Is she still trying to decide if this is her brother or just the shell? Has hope just blinded her?

Lloyd continues to stare at me. His smile is set, like a question that hangs. But if I had remained at Carlsbad since Visitation, perhaps I too would be like this man – blank and diminished.

Just as the silence between us grows uncomfortable, a movement at the dark recesses of the cave catches my eye.

A woman steps unsteadily from the gloom. Lank red hair, welts on her arms, dazed eyes. A mist of defeat hangs over her.

'Christ, I nearly forgot!' exclaims Kelly. 'Always reckoned these two had a thing going. This is Melissa Mumford. Partner in crime at the Taco-Shack-O, ain't that right, Mumps? Cemetery shift. Always plotting our escape to the City of Angels, huh? In between getting our asses pinched and stealin' each other's tips.'

A slight frown passes across Melissa Mumford's face as if this did indeed happen but she had forgotten. Kelly gazes at me pointedly, as if to say, *This is the proof. Teenage sweethearts. Don't you see? How could they be Visitors? They're like us. They're human.*

Just when I think no one apart from Kelly will speak, her brother says, 'We been here three years now.'

'And we're gonna get you outta here, ain't that true, Megan?'

Before I can answer, Kelly drops to her knees beside me. Something has cracked inside her as if now, after hours of trying, she has just realised that the chasm between her and these people is unbridgeable.

'And Mom?' Her voice wavers but in the demand there is anger too. 'Pop? How come you ain't said nothing? They come with you? When d'you last see them? It's all right now if it's bad news. You can just tell me, can't you?'

But they can't. They have no understanding of family. They don't remember anything about Valentine life or Kelly. She has filled in their memories for them, in the desperate hope they will recognise her. I see it in their faces now – so passive. They are not like the Visitors we have seen before – the outlaws, aping emotion and speech patterns in an effort to disguise their otherness. It is as if Carlsbad has drained them of the will.

They share a glance then, as if trying to recover some remnant of their previous existence. And perhaps there are wisps of memory – dry, like shapes in fossilised brains. A recognition does pass between them, I think. A charge. It reminds me of something . . . And as one they turn their empty gazes upon me.

ANGELS OF WAR

Kelly edges away from them, no longer in denial.

I am riveted for a moment by their faces. Lloyd's smile slackens at last.

Fragments of thought fly at me then, all at once, as though flushed from the places they've been hiding. Things which would go together if only I could focus: hawks hovering for the kill; a funnel of bats . . . *so dense*; Cisco galloping through his dreams out there beyond my reach; these human husks before me. How is it possible we have found them? From Kelly's disappeared home town? Here? Now? Kelly's breathless question – *What are the frickin' chances?* It cannot be chance. The Zone is not fertile ground for coincidence like this. It is a huge wilderness . . . almost boundless, and cruel. We were sent here. I think of Pa's message – his smell coming to me so strongly in the cave. The clues to escape are all around. Bats . . . never straying from each other on their tight course to and from the cave. Hawks never alighting on dangerous ground. I feel then that I am looking the wrong way, that I should be facing the swarm behind me. So measured as they come home to roost! Not returning from all directions as you would expect . . . As though they are following a trail.

But I don't turn. I cannot. Pa! It is the only explanation that makes sense. He has guided me here to this special place, this miniature zone within a zone. It is a test I must overcome. Some truth I must grasp. The key to our safe passage from Carlsbad is right before my eyes. So it must be for the wider Zone, isn't that the message? Navigation depends on mastery, understanding of the Zone. If only I try hard enough to see. *Here secrets are unveiled in the darkness.*

Of course . . . Kelly is no different to Luis. She came on this journey not for me, but to find her family. She could not stay in our room at the Drunken Steer because she was desperate to look for them, desperate for any clue to their whereabouts . . . She pushed and cajoled for us to go to Brokeoff in the first instance, to where people live. The poker game was just a chance for her to examine the locals of the saloon.

I lift my eyes again to Lloyd and I know now what I am

reminded of. It is the same electric unease I felt in the presence of the Visitor back at Marfa – Jethro's outlaw, the one known as Bud Haslett, striding through the sheriff's office towards me.

The same terrible visions flash through my mind as they did that day and I can do nothing to control them. It is not just a warning. It is happening now. At the dark heart of the Zone. *People all in a row, waiting until light swallows them and they scream without sound, their mouths hinged back, jaws breaking right open, their faces unfurling like dreadful flowers . . .*

'Megan?' whispers Kelly. 'Megan?'

The urge to reach out and touch the Visitors is irresistible.

My outstretched fingers tremble.

The Lloyd Visitor lifts a hand.

The palm opens, like a greeting, like an acceptance. And the lines that fortune-tellers read just peel apart. Flesh petals. No blood. Just the forever twining of blue strands where bones and tendons should be. They glow slightly, illuminating the dust between us. Dry as grass. Slipping and twisting and weaving. A stream of elver flowing to the fingers.

'Jesus! Megan!'

Kelly tugs me back.

The Lloyd one is old. Incredibly old. I see it behind those stolen eyes, dead as baubles. The gold of fires – unimaginably far away.

The shining blue threads of its true being are cold. And as I touch them, a flame tears through my heart.

Visions blast into me. The Visitors hold nothing back.

I see who they are and what they have done.

Worlds uncounted have fallen to their kind. I see their distant homes in banded skies of russet and carmine, storms the size of the Earth that last a thousand years. They are angels of war. They are nothing like people. And we will not be spared. Not a single soul.

I am so cold. Thoughts plod around my brain in a senseless procession. I gaze into the fire of their eyes, these unknowable creatures, and remember the settler family at Fort Davis – all kneeling at the end of their lives. I am to be frozen, as they were.

I try to break away but it is impossible now. I am caught in the thrall of blue fibres. They snake about my wrist, as strong as creeper vines that have grown there over centuries.

Kelly's screams are desperate but they remain far, far away.

What is it that saves me? Surely not mercy. They don't know what it means. It is their nature to occupy, to lay waste, to move onto unchartered worlds in relentless hunger. Like a disease.

Not mercy. Weakness? They withdraw suddenly as if repelled by something. They stare at me through slack faces. They know they cannot escape the sinkhole of Carlsbad. They have hidden these three years, cornered inside sick and starving bodies, trapped as helplessly as everyone else here, and now they will be exposed for what they are.

I stagger away from their touch. My arm flops numb and useless. Spikes of frost like chilblains dig about my shoulder. I snatch at the air, knowing I must breathe, but with each tiny lungful I feel only closer to suffocation.

Kelly drags me clear. She is yelling at me, at them. A terrified stream of obscenities. At last my chest opens and I draw down air – sweet and warm. The Visitors observe the commotion before them in complete detachment. As aloof and still as effigies in a tomb. Their *otherness* has left me stunned. It is as though I have been submerged into a world where every single living thing is prey.

Kelly lifts up a rock, ready to cast it. But there's more sorrow in her than anger. She is torn. She cannot strike against those that resemble her kin. And she cannot even guess at how removed they are from the Lloyd and Melissa she once knew. They await their fate calmly, gazing past us without fear towards the shouting of a mob.

I scramble out of the cave mouth into weak sunshine. And there, charging across the rocks is Luis, shoving people aside to reach us. He arrives first, hauls me to my feet and yells at Kelly to retreat. But there is nowhere to flee, we are at the edge of Carlsbad. Sleep laps at our backs.

I am transfixed then, unable to look away. The Visitors turn and clasp each other by the hands and kneel. The petals of skin peel away from their knuckles to reveal all the strands of their true being, twined together. An icy blue light blasts out from the union of their fibres. And in an instant it is snuffed out. What remains are two fixed husks, facing each other, coated in thick frost, frozen solid.

Kelly buckles and falls to the ground. Whatever tiny hope she has been clinging to, that her brother can be resurrected somehow, has been crushed. All she can do is look at me and howl.

I take one arm, Luis takes the other – we lift her as gently as we can and face back up the gulley.

A crowd of Carlsbad inhabitants has gathered there. They are armed with rocks. At their head stands Wesley Carmichael. I see it in all their faces, in the way they have no need of words. We are to be stoned. We have consorted with Visitors. There will be no trial. They wait only for his command.

Only then do I look again at the sky, at the dark spiral arm of bats above the cavern maw. A hawk hovers there above its prey, taking care not to stray beyond the limits of the multitude.

And then I have it.

It is so simple.

There is a trail that leads out of this place. One that opens twice a day. With the coming and going of the bats. They lead the way. That is why they funnel so closely across the sky in a black ribbon.

And any creature may follow it.

I glance once to the road. It is shrouded in the shadow of ten million bats. And there pushing himself to a groggy standing position is Cisco.

Wesley Carmichael raises his hand. It is the signal of our execution.

I turn to the others, haul down the biggest breath my lungs will take and bellow at them.

'RUN!'

A SILENT TOAST

I hurtle down the gulley. Luis is beside me as the first rocks rain down from above. As I risk a glance back, missiles thud at my feet. For a dreadful moment I cannot see Kelly – I imagine her locked by the sight of the dead Visitors, unable to flee. But she flings herself down the scree just as the sky is suddenly blurred with flying stones. One smacks my hat off and I snatch it up from the dry streambed as we reach the first cover of bushes and trees.

The bats are not directly overhead and straight away I feel the draw of sleep. It sends my head into stars like the dull surprise of concussion. Kelly staggers into me.

'Follow the bats.' My words take an age to launch.

Stones plock into the branches, but the salvo is lessening. Perhaps our pursuers are content to watch the Zone sleep take us. The very ground drifts away as my mind clouds over. I grasp about for my companions and stumble towards the flittering noise of bats. Only that sound, that rippling river of wings can save us . . .

And then, as one might gasp from a drowning nightmare, I start up. The air is dark above me, and all about the dirt shadows run. Kelly and Luis are just behind me, propping each other up, ducking beneath a fine drizzle of guano.

We scramble up onto the road and Cisco is there turning in bewilderment, twitching with energy. My beloved horse! I hold my head against his in prayer and thanks.

'Can we save the lovin' up 'til we get clear of them sons of bitches?' Kelly yells at me.

She has a point – it will only be a matter of time before the prisoners of Carlsbad see that they are prisoners no more. The other horses are further up the trail, nosing about for water but none the worse for wear. We mount up, taking care to follow the bats as they veer northwards, away from the road, carving a safe passage through the sleeping sickness.

I glance at Kelly, but she will not hold my eye. Now that the worst of the danger is past, her face is blank and shattered. She has borne the hardest news – that her brother is dead, and that, in all likelihood, so are the rest of her family.

The returning bats pick a route through low mountain

passes, holding tight to their formation. A dead air hangs over the country. No insects stir in the grasses. For some ten miles as we thread our way out of the Guadalupe range, I feel the sleep holding the land in its grip like a quiet winter. But at last, in the dry scrub north of the mountains, the funnel of bats thins out as they are free to fly anywhere. The throb of crickets winds up and that oppressive atmosphere of sleep evaporates.

We reach a sharp drop in the land – a rim of rock that levels out into a featureless basin far below. Great stretches of New Mexico roll out to the western skies, aflame with afternoon gold. I think of it then, this world, drawn through the heavens, captive to its fate, like a long-horn bull cut from the herd. Dragged and goaded to slaughter.

There is a Zone stillness at this overlook. It is a place to take stock. Horse tails flick at the flies. We each gaze at the sky, in exhaustion at the forces that have washed us up here, like shipwrecked sailors. Blood pounds through my head and in the breeze I hear brief snatches of thunder – horses galloping. But we are alone here. Out across the plain, between blinks, I see something I know isn't there. A distant mass of graves beyond counting. Headstones dissolve into nothing. For a moment, it feels like the Zone and my mind are the same thing. Another clue, another message.

Kelly dismounts, swaying slightly, as if the ground is not fixed. She begins to gather stones, planting them into a careful pile at the very edge of the overlook. She considers each stone, which has lain here in all probability untouched by human fingers. The chip and scrape of their surfaces makes a dry clatter on the wind.

After some minutes, I join her, balancing more stones into a precarious cairn that rises to my waist. Luis, too, helps shore up the base, scouting over the ridge for suitable rocks. It is a nameless act of remembrance and I am sure it means a different thing to each of us. A way to make a simple mark on the landscape. A way to further seal our pact. A way to say goodbye to lost ones. Kelly says nothing. Her eyes glisten in the sun as she takes a ring from her thumb and buries it in the gaps between stones. There will be no body, or marker, or clue to why the cairn stands. Perhaps no one will pass this way again, let alone find the ring, or wonder at its meaning.

We stand around it for a while. A hawk cries somewhere, thin and insistent. Kelly passes around her silver hip flask and we each take a nip of the liquor – a silent toast to what lies behind, what lies ahead.

Kelly is the first to break away. 'Well, then. Let's get this show on the road.'

She pulls the Rand McNally from my pack.

The sick realisation dawns on us all – that the hand-drawn map my aunt gave me has gone. I remember it being snatched by the Visitor after we left Brokeoff. In the confusion and drama of these past hours I have paid it no attention.

'I should have committed its details to memory, I should have destroyed it . . .'

'Maybe this Visitor he still sleeps,' says Luis.

'And maybe not. We were driven to Carlsbad – the

175

Zone forces that bore the sleep were on the move. In which case, the Visitor may only have been under their spell for a short time.'

Kelly says nothing. If she had killed the Visitor, the map would now be hidden on a corpse. Instead, if he survived the Zone sleep, it is likely now to have fallen into the hands of our enemies.

'That Visitor was making a rendezvous with others in the gang,' I murmur. 'Jethro will have it.'

'You don't know that,' replies Kelly.

'We have to assume it. I told the Visitor about Spider Rock, the cemetery. They know what we know.'

'Then we gotta get there first, huh?' says Kelly. 'Beat 'em to it.'

I think then about the thundering hooves, the graves beyond number, my dream of Pa in the stagecoach.

'No, we have to find the Mavis Pilgrim. It'll tell us which grave to look for.'

Kelly leafs quickly through the Rand McNally. 'It's a mail-run, right? Between Hope and Truth or Consequences. It must take the 82 west up through Cloudcroft if it sticks to roads. That's what . . . thirty miles north of here.'

'Sí, but when?' groans Luis. 'Is one in a week, a month?'

'What day is it today? Anyone keepin' count? Cos may as well be Judgment Day for all I know.'

'Is Tuesday.'

'Day, night?'

I consult my pocket watch. 'A quarter after ten – evening. Why?'

'Cos Josie bailed someone out in that poker game at the saloon. Remember Mr Zit-face, in the shades? Ten decent hands in a row, but he weren't smart enough to do a damn thing with 'em.'

I have a vague recollection of the characters at the poker table. 'So?'

'He begged Josie to sub him. She weren't interested – said it was good money after bad. But he kept on – said he'd do anything. Turns out he ain't got the head for cards but he was the best rider in Brokeoff by a country mile. Barrel-racer back in the day. County champion. Josie loaned him sixty bucks if he agreed to ride to Hope to catch the mail-run before it set out Wednesday. She's got a sister in Truth or Consequences or wherever. Wants her to help run the saloon. Ask me, she didn't need no help . . .' Kelly throws a play punch at Luis. 'There, ain't you glad you put up with me and my gamblin' ways?'

'So, what time does the Mavis Pilgrim leave Hope tomorrow?' I ask.

Kelly shrugs. 'They never said.'

'Maybe could be any time,' says Luis. 'From midnight.'

I spare a glance for the barren country along the ridge. 'That's less than two hours. If it leaves at the first opportunity on Wednesday we'd never reach Hope in time.'

'So? We just follow the trail from there and catch it up,' suggests Kelly.

I shake my head. 'You're forgetting the Jethro Gang. If they know about the stagecoach run, they'll be all along the road lying in wait for it.'

'Seems to me we've gotta do the same,' says Kelly

firmly. 'Trouble is, where?'

I consult the atlas. 'If you wanted to hold up a stagecoach, where's the best place for an ambush?'

Luis points with his finger. 'Here. Before the mountains. Not in open.'

'Nice one,' murmurs Kelly. 'Hole up in some pass with a good view of the road back down to the plain. Spring them before they can turn back. Your money or your life, then off into the hills.'

I look at Kelly and Luis as they nod in deep agreement. And I am slightly alarmed at the ease with which they have taken on the mind-set of criminals.

Kelly slams the atlas shut. 'Just gotta hope we get to it before Jethro does.'

THE MAVIS PILGRIM

I am beset with worry – worry that the Zone will throw obstacles in our path, that we will be waylaid and miss the stagecoach, that Jethro will intercept the Mavis Pilgrim before us. Also, both Luis and Kelly's horses are Visitor steeds, marked with scorpion brands. If I'm right about the way the Visitor at Brokeoff tracked us down, the horses can be traced from afar. But we have no choice – speed is paramount now.

The stagecoach schedule must necessarily be a hazy affair for there are no certainties in the Zone. It cannot even follow a fixed route given the dangers it must face. I wonder how many times it has disappeared without trace – its crew must be drawn from brave and resourceful trackers. Despite my worries, however, the Zone remains quiet and the night's ride passes without serious incident.

We follow the rim of rock in a north-westerly arc until it peters out into flatter country. Here the Pinon Drunken Road meets Highway 82 as it begins its climb into the mountains of Lincoln Forest.

At three in the morning we come to a steep-sided pass as good as any, veering off-road a way for a clear view eastwards down onto the plain, where hopefully the Mavis Pilgrim will appear. We wait in silence, taking turns to doze and keep watch. The sun strikes only the highest ramparts of the rock above. The pink stone bristles with thorn bushes. The gorge road directly below is filled with shadow as it always must be.

The morning drags by. Now that we've stopped moving it is perishing cold. I can't even feel the chattering teeth in my mouth. For hours I stare at the surrounding country, but there is not a soul out there, just a pair of buzzards circling the crown of rock above us.

In my head, I rehearse violent encounters with Visitor outlaws. I lose count of the times I load the Colt revolver in proper fashion. It weighs heavy on my belt. I am not confident. Firing at cans back in Marfa doesn't amount to much practice. Especially as I wasn't liable to hit any of them.

It is Luis who has the keenest eyes. I squint in the direction of his pointed finger. Some way north of Highway 82, in the distance – a puff of red dust on the open desert.

I lean on an outcrop to steady the view through my spyglass.

It has to be the Mavis, though I can't make it out yet – just a billowing cloud on the edge of haze. But it's moving in a fearsome hurry. And that's got to be bad news.

There! In the slanting gold light, I see a brace of lead horses and the driver on his box. He's standing, whipping his team to kingdom come. Next to him, crouches one of the Mavis minders, carbine at the ready, leaning back to aim. I see the barrel kick then the shot rings out across the plain.

Jethro's gang has got there before us.

Now I see them, four outriders at least. They're hammering up on either side, taking aim at the driver.

Kelly snatches the spyglass from me. 'There's only four,' she says.

I snatch it back. '*Only* four?'

'We need whatever's on that stagecoach, Megan,' she says grimly.

I can hear the barest rumble now, of hooves and screaming.

We cannot just watch this raid unfold . . .

But there are four outlaw Visitors, maybe more in their wake, and they will not take kindly to a rival bid.

We must choose. We must choose now. I spring onto Cisco.

Lord help us and keep our souls. A quick glance at my companions and I know they are with me.

Neckerchief up over my mouth. Well, I'm a bandit now! I jam the spyglass into my pouch, grab the reins and pull Cisco round to face the scree. It's a steep ride and I'm practically lying down with my boots scraping Cisco's withers as he slides into deepest shadow.

We all hit the base of the gorge together and fly out at full tilt into the forever sunset. The Mavis is maybe half a mile away. It careens and bobs as the lead horses charge into open country littered with boulders and mesquites. The driver hasn't seen us, I'm sure. He is too busy with the marauders to the left and right. They foray in and out, taking turns to come in for a potshot, and I'm pretty sure they haven't seen us either.

I stand into the stirrups and fumble for my Colt, though I've never felt less ready to fire it. But now as the Mavis Pilgrim closes on us, I glance at Luis and Kelly on either side of me and I feel a hot rush of blood. We are locked. We cannot waver now. What is this? A death charge? Cisco does not baulk so he must feel it too.

Gunfire cracks the air.

The dust cloud ahead is a storm rising high. The raiders dart in and out of it. Their whoops clamour over the cascade of hooves and we're close enough to see the rolling shoulders of all four team horses. They have blinkers but surely they've seen us by now. The rifleman on the driver's box lands a shot that wings one of the outriders. It doesn't seem real the way the outlaw snaps clean out of his saddle and over the rump of his horse. He's lost in the dust.

With perhaps two hundred metres to go, I find that I'm screaming. My hat flies back and the tie practically garrottes me. Sweet Jesus of Nazareth, is the driver blind?

I point the Colt skyward and pull the trigger once.

Nothing.

Some bandit I turned out to be.

But then I remember. I haven't cocked it.

The Mavis team pulls a thunderhead of dust. We'll be mangled to dog meat.

The Colt is so big I've never managed to cock it with anything other than two thumbs. I stuff the reins into my teeth, just my thighs holding me on now. Yank back the hammer and . . . fire!

The recoil nearly unseats me.

I see the glint of the driver's hat badge when he finally realises what he's riding into.

No time for pulling up. He careers the team to our right, throwing the brake as he goes. The swerve is so sudden he clips one of the outriders whose horse goes down.

The noise of the carriage thudding through the scrub is terrible. One rear wheel cracks up and clear, spraying its spokes in a high arc. The coach body twists and ploughs over, pulling the horses into a heap. Cisco bucks as I steer him round, and straight into the path of a raider. He yells something as he spots me. Does he mistake me for one of his party? There's no time to change direction. I lift the Colt as he brushes by, and clout him full-face with the butt. My wrist snaps back with the force. There's a surprised grunt and a thud as he hits the ground.

Everywhere is churning dirt and for a moment I can't see Kelly or Luis. I counted four riders so there's one more in the melee somewhere. I swing Cisco into tight circles, trying to balance the gun in my left. I can't even shoot straight with my right, so this should be interesting.

There, a shadow slumped on horseback, picking its way towards the coach wreckage. He does not see me. His interest lies only with the spinning wheels of the carriage, the muffled yells from the passengers inside. He levels a pistol as he walks his horse closer. And as the dust clears I see it is the same Visitor from Brokeoff.

Only now does the pain surge through my wrist, but I do not think it's broken, or I would not even be able to flex it.

I steady my Colt and cock it again.

'Back up.' I put as much gruff in the words as I can, and I try to damp down the terror in my heart.

He straightens, raising both hands. But he doesn't let go of his gun.

'Drop the piece, and back up.'

'Whatever you find in this stagecoach,' he growls. 'It won't save you. Or your friends.'

'I said to drop the gun. And if you say another word I'll shoot you anyhow.'

I bring Cisco close in. Even I can't miss from here.

He dangles his gun by the trigger guard and lets it fall.

I reach in with my bad hand and pinch out his other pistol from its holster, casting it behind me.

The passengers inside the carriage are silent now.

I can sense him going through his options, weighing up what I will do now, whether I'm capable of pulling the trigger.

He says, 'We know where you're headed. Canyon de

Chelly. Spider Rock.'

Well, I did warn him. And I've got to do something. So I line up the Colt with the top of his hat and fire. The Stetson flies off in tatters and his horse gives a mighty start. For good measure I jab its rump with my spurs and he's off. I reckon it's a good thirty metres before he gets the horse even half under control but then he doesn't look back, just hightails north across the desert.

I turn to see Kelly and Luis checking on the other three riders – either laid out cold or dead, I can't tell which.

'Nice one, Megan,' says Kelly. 'How we gonna win this war when you keep saving their asses?' But there's a hint of respect in her voice too. Because between us we have faced them down, and survived intact.

The driver and the rifleman must be hunkered down on the far side of the Mavis. The horses have broken their traces and are wandering out in the scrub.

'Stand down,' I cry. 'The outlaws are scattered.' I don't know what else to say, and now that the immediate danger has passed I begin to shake uncontrollably.

A head pokes up behind the carriage roof. 'Identify yourself!'

I swing down from Cisco and rip the neckerchief clear.

'Goddamn it, Hogart!' cries a voice almost beside itself with rage. 'Is that a girl?'

'There's not a moment to lose,' I call out. 'We will not harm you, but we must search this stagecoach. Then we will be on our way.'

Nobody moves.

Kelly cocks her rifle. 'You heard the lady. Move your butts.'

'Goddamn it all to hell – is that another girl?'

In an angry sing-song voice Kelly says, 'Yep, two girls and we've both got guns with proper bullets in and we've had a real bad couple of days. Oh, and my buddy Luis – he's nearly as dangerous as a *girl*. So, let's cut the crap and hustle it along here.'

THE BRIDGWATER POSSE

The coach driver lets forth a cascade of blasphemies that would curl the toes of Lucifer himself. He pauses only to spit black chaw juice from the wad of tobacco that rests in one bulging cheek.

'Since when in this godforsaken land did girls knee-high to a chipmunk start holding up mail routes?'

I paraphrase, for this man's words cannot be repeated in polite company.

'We're not holding anything up.' I look at my

companions and gesture for them to take down their bandit masks. 'There is something in the stagecoach . . . Something that belongs to me.'

The other man, Hogart, the one who rode shotgun with the driver, delivers a look of sneering contempt. 'Well, if it ain't a hold-up, thank Mother Mary.'

Then he saunters over to the body of the nearest bandit and pumps a round in his head to make sure.

'Hey!' I cry. 'Put your gun down!'

Hogart eyes me with cold disgust. 'Quit yer bellyachin' – they'da killed every last one of us. Law of the Zone.' He raises his voice for the driver, all the while glaring at me. 'Fetch up them horses, Colson! One of 'em bad boys got away and I ain't keen for them takin' a second bite of the cherry. This here's the Jethro Gang – dead or alive, the Justice of the Peace ain't choosy.'

He begins to rifle through the dead bandit's possessions.

Colson, the driver, pipes up. 'Hey, I want my share of pickings!'

'If you don't get them horses hitched up and righting this wagon, I'll testify you ran it off trail without due reason. We had 'em licked 'til you lost your nerve.'

The driver glares at me, but you can tell he's kowtowed. He stomps off to retrieve his horses, spitting profanities and jets of dark saliva.

'Y'all just break out the freak farm?' cries Kelly. She fires her rifle in the air. 'Seeing as playin' nice ain't working out real good let's start all over.'

'So it is a hold-up anyhow,' Hogart mocks. 'Well, Lord

have mercy.'

He pauses over another slumped outlaw and guns him between the eyes. As three we level our guns at Hogart as he strides over to the last hapless bandit.

'Pull that trigger one more time,' warns Kelly. 'And I'll send you straight to hell.'

'Make your mind up, sweetheart. Either it's a stick-up or it ain't.'

Kelly looks at me in disbelief. This man is either insane or drunk or pitifully stupid. Perhaps he is all three.

''Cos if it is a stick-up, I'm handing you over to the sheriff's office just as soon as we make Truth.'

I look at the revolting specimen that is the Mavis Pilgrim gun-for-hire.

'Under whose authority?' I demand.

'Under the authority of Presidio County law. I deputise for the sheriff on any and every stagecoach leg that takes in Zone territory.' He heaves up a lungful of phlegm and shoots it into the dust. 'Hell, I don't need no authority. Not for no busybody kids who ain't got no federal permit to be here.'

I am at a loss. This man is a lunatic. He looks at the chambers of his gun and frowns, then starts to pick bullets out of his belt to reload.

'What we've got here is a citizen's arrest,' he warns. 'Damage of company property, delay of the county mail service . . . hell, who's to say you ain't in cahoots with them Jethro boys? Holdin' up the Pilgrim. I'd be in my rights to shoot all three of you if you was thinking of resisting arrest.'

What? Trust us to pick a stagecoach manned by a belligerent oaf. But he is certainly cold-blooded enough to shoot us if he believes in his tin-pot jurisdiction. He seems in no hurry at all to load the gun, even taking time to blow dust from the barrel.

'That is a preposterous charge,' I bluster. 'Made by a man ignorant in the extreme. If it wasn't for us you'd be meat for the buzzards.'

'Well, let's see now. Riding full pelt at a registered stagecoach.' He glances at Kelly. 'With *real* guns and *real* bullets.' He gestures at said stagecoach lying in pieces.

It is at that precise moment that Kelly sees red. It has been brewing but Hogart has steadfastly refused to see it coming.

'Kelly . . .'

He is droning on about the state of company property when Kelly lines her rifle up with the man's toe-cap and fires. In the shock before pain he stares at Kelly and faints.

'Right,' she shouts at the upturned stagecoach. 'This is a robbery. Sorry for the inconvenience'n'all but if you don't line up out here at the count of five then I'm gonna get all trigger-happy on your ass. One, two . . .'

When I look over at Colson, the driver, he has unhitched one of the horses and is galloping back towards the road.

The occupants of the Mavis Pilgrim emerge, disorientated and in silence. There is a man I know to be a priest from Alpine, who is no doubt on a mission in the Zone to save souls. By his dejected demeanour and cracked spectacles I'm guessing his haul for the Lord has been a disappointing one. Two women clutch each other and cast wild glances at us and the wreckage of the Mavis. Their saloon bar petticoats and coiffed hair mark them out as entertainers, of ill repute I daresay, on their way to Truth or Consequences. What they'll find there is anyone's guess. Consequences probably. The final passenger has a tasselled jacket in the style of a frontiersman, steel-tipped collars in his shirt and a wide-brimmed hat. They are the clothes of a tourist – a man who pays for a taste of the Zone, but stays in safe guest houses and exaggerates his exploits in a journal. I have seen many such travellers in Marfa, who gawp at the Deadline checkpoint and consider themselves adventurers for reaching a place where their portable telephones cease to operate.

I feel as though I am on the wrong track. None of these people look like regular travellers into the Zone. How can they possibly be holding a clue, wittingly or unwittingly, to my father's whereabouts? I glance at the others to cover me as I begin to ransack through the scattered trunks and bags.

There is a meek protest from the tourist but he holds his tongue when Kelly tells him to. His lack of courage is curiously at odds with his frontiersman jacket.

The contents of the luggage are ordinary enough: underwear, spare clothes, Zone papers. I have no idea what I'm looking for.

'Is maybe in the carriage, Megan,' suggests Luis. 'The map say Mavis Pilgrim. Passenger come, passenger go.'

'Yeah, look for something hidden inside, under the

seats or whatever,' says Kelly.

'Who are you?' asks the fake frontiersman timidly.

'The Bridgwater Posse,' drawls Kelly in irritation. 'Who the hell are you?'

'Bridgwater? You're M-Megan,' he stutters at me. 'Virgil Bridgwater's girl.'

I stare at him. 'What do you know of my pa?'

He tries to smile. 'I'm a writer, well, a journalist really.' He holds out a shaking hand that I do not take. 'Gallop. Joshua Gallop. Sort of a pen name actually. Look at my papers. That's my profession. It says right there. I write about the Zone. Well, I'd like to go further than Truth but it's far too dangerous you see. So, I talk to the inhabitants there, find out their stories. Then I-I head back to Hope on the stagecoach and out of the Zone so I can wire it all back east. It's terribly popular, tales of derring-do and the like. People can't get enough of it – adventures from the wild frontier et cetera et cetera. I take this route whenever it runs . . .'

'Goddamn it, Gallop. Megan's daddy – cut to the chase, eh?'

'Oh yes, of course.' He mops his brow even though it is too cold for perspiration. 'Well, I suppose it's really rather bad news, you could say. You see, Virgil Bridgwater is d-dead.'

I stare at him in a daze, unable to speak, unable to think.

Gallop gabbles on, anxious to fill the silence. 'An old Indian tracker told me about a month ago at the T&C saloon – one that partnered up with your father on several expeditions, a man called Yiska, I believe. To tell you the truth I rather dismissed his account at first. He was somewhat incoherent, spoke in riddles mostly. Nonetheless all the saloon regulars paid him a great deal of respect. Yiska showed me a map – hand-drawn, a little worse for wear. Said he knew of the grave up at a cemetery in Canyon de Chelly, near a place called . . . Dear me, what was the name of it?'

'Spider Rock,' answers Kelly in a dead voice.

Gallop looks briefly delighted. 'Yes, that's it. Spider Rock.' Something like belated sorrow enters his face as he turns to me. 'Please accept my c-condolences on your loss.'

I look into the middle distance. At nothing but featureless land. And I crumple inside.

WHERE LAND RIVERS BEGIN

Voices are raised around me.

    I hear but I don't listen.

I am thinking of an untended grave somewhere far away in the lee of a canyon wall.

I have been fooling myself. I have been reading the Zone all wrong. My pa is dead.

Kelly is shouting at the other passengers to leave. There is weeping from the entertainer women. They clutch at the silk and velvet frocks that limp across the land, scattered to the wind. The priest has taken to praying. Kelly yells at them that outlaws from another planet will return soon and that they will be frozen to death or worse if they don't take the remaining three horses and head out of the Zone. Joshua Gallop complains that he cannot ride. Kelly bellows that he'd better learn 'real quick'. Hogart has regained consciousness but stays silent. Disarmed and crippled, he lies propped up against the wreckage of the Mavis, seemingly resigned to his fate.

Luis speaks to me softly, in Spanish. 'Megan, we must leave. Jethro will be back for the whereabouts of the grave.'

The whereabouts of the grave. All this time I have been working my way towards what? The plain fact of my father's death. It seems unreservedly cruel, even for the Zone.

Luis takes my hand. 'If your father draw this map, then he is alive, no?'

A simple deduction. How would a dead man be able to direct you to his own grave, unless he had returned from the dead?

'The map can't be from him,' I reply. 'Yiska must have drawn it. He must have come to Marfa, to tell my aunt.'

'But she said Señor Bridgwater is alive.'

'There was no signature on that map. If it was truly from him, why would he not write to me? It would have been easy.'

'It was made in a hurry. Perhaps he could not. To put his mark on it makes the map precious, dangerous . . .'

So many questions unanswered.

What is not in doubt is that we have uncovered the intended clue. This is not coincidence. Whoever made the map knew of Gallop, of his frequent trips via this stagecoach, and knew that Gallop was a wealth of knowledge about the Zone, about Virgil Bridgwater.

The secret of the Zone, the secret of our salvation, whatever it might be, still lies in that grave. With or without the bones of my poor father. It is only this that makes me rise at last on legs that have no strength.

With Luis I round up the three stray team horses. There is no reasoning with the passengers of the ill-fated Mavis, so we practically saddle them at gunpoint like sacks of provisions. The women wail as their horse bears them in aimless fashion in the general direction of Hope. The priest flops like a straw scarecrow on his steed. Only the Lord's Prayer and Luis's knots keep him from a tumble. Hogart won't be goaded or cajoled. He stares at us and the final horse in an impassive way as if his last spark of reason has departed for the wilderness.

We ride in silence back into the Sacramento Mountains. I have never seen such fertile country. The ground is lush, running with creeks and rich with grasses. Dismounting, I let poor Cisco rest and stock up. Everywhere is wet, and soft with soaked mosses. Sharp showers fall through pines as we climb higher to Cloudcroft. Toffee-coloured cicadas cling to every scrap of bark, scratching a chorus that drowns out the rain.

The town of Cloudcroft is derelict and mouldering – log cabins collapsing in on themselves and clogged with ferns. We proceed cautiously, guns at the ready, but there are no signs of Jethro's gang.

We share a can of beans on the hoof, and in a break of the clouds I spot the White Sands in Tularosa Valley twenty-five miles away, like a bright vein of silver before the shadow of the San Andres Mountains.

'Where the sheriff he say to ride, eh, Megan?' remarks Luis. 'White Sands. Some tracker there . . .'

'Devon Marshall.'

White Sands has not figured in my plans, but Zone plans rarely come to pass. And our diversion to Carlsbad makes the place difficult to avoid now. If we are to reach our ultimate destination at Canyon de Chelly, White Sands is our next port of call.

'He lives there – the desert?' asks Luis.

I shrug. 'I have not heard of trackers ever making a home.' I think of my pa as I say this. 'At least not in the Zone.'

'We gonna look him up, this Marshall?' says Kelly. 'I mean, he could be handy to have on board.'

'The Visitor at Brokeoff mentioned White Sands also, for all those travelling north,' I reply. 'A bottleneck in the Zone perhaps? He talked of land rivers, though I have not heard of them. They are not marked on my map.'

'Something new?' suggests Kelly.

'The Zone is always changing.'

I pick up the pace, eager to make distance while my Zone quivers are quiet. 'Bottlenecks are dangerous because every traveller must gather there. But maybe we do not have a choice.'

We follow the 82 west but come to an unmarked tunnel at the edge of the mountains. I am reluctant to be enclosed in such a place, but finding an alternative way down to the desert flats will take precious time. The dark is forbidding and filled with wind echoes. But our minds are made when the rain turns to fat flakes of snow – it is too cold to tarry in these mountains. The horses do not like the tunnel, but no harm comes to us, and when we emerge at last into clear light it is as though we have passed through into another world, so drastic is the change in climate.

The air is powder dry. Shimmering desert stretches out before us. The old towns of La Luz and Alamogordo are scoured of life and seem destined to be buried under a blanket of sand. Car showroom signs poke from the drifts like tomb markers.

There is an air of perpetual restlessness about the land here and I raise my guard. We cross the runway at Holloman Air Force Base – a graveyard of fighter jets upended by unknown forces.

Since the flight from Carlsbad, we have been riding the whole night and most of the day and we are exhausted by the time we reach the first drifts of white gypsum. The grit hisses around the horses' hooves, gusting up into our faces, but it is a magical, impossible place. Great fin-shaped ridges like ocean breakers climb into the air casting violet shadows and throwing tails of dust from their overhangs.

Perhaps it is the whipping of the wind that blinds us to the true nature of White Sands. Cisco senses it first – the way his legs sink and are carried. It is not just the surface that is unstable, it is the entire procession of dunes. The whole desert is moving gently in vast slow-motion ripples.

I cry out to the others but somehow the sensation is not alarming.

Luis has dismounted and wades up to his knees. He smiles at me. 'Try it!'

Just for a few moments, my troubles drop away. We glance at each other floundering in the sand, pouring it through our fingers. For the fun of it. I feel light, almost weightless. It's as though the trials of the journey that brought us to this place cease to matter. We are here. We are alive. We are friends. I close my eyes but when I open them again Luis's carefree smile has gone. His look is searching, loaded somehow with a meaning that escapes me.

Kelly bobs by on an upwelling of new sand – it spills about her and bears her along. The horses splay and turn in lazy currents. We are sent to the crest of a gigantic bank and from there, as we tip, I can see the margins of the desert flowing out into a dozen or so spokes. They run into canyons at the outset of the San Andres Mountains, carving sheer slots from the rock. They are the land rivers and we are at their source.

Further north I watch great gouts of dust blasting into the sky – geysers massing into white pillars, fanning and bursting in the wind.

And, as if issuing from a wondrous dream, perched upon the flow of one mighty land river, I see a wooden house. It pitches and yaws, anchored to static boulders by a series of chains. In clumsy wading bounds I am reunited with Cisco, for it is not difficult to navigate the currents.

By and by, we converge upon the floating house. Smoke escapes from an iron chimney. A man stands up from his easy chair on the back porch. He waves us around to a log pier tacked onto one side of the house where one raggedy mule is tied up. From here he helps us guide the horses out of the river.

He is a small man, but I feel his great strength as he hauls me aboard the creaking planks. His face is much weathered by the wind, like wood that has split with age, but his eyes are bright and friendly. He touches the peak of a baseball cap that says simply, 'I'm older'.

'Howdy, Ma'am.'

'You're Devon Marshall.'

'The same. If we been acquainted you'd have to remind me of it. I ain't used to folks out here. But I'm mighty glad of the company. Shot me a brace of wild turkeys and they're roastin' pretty fine. The Lord knows how they came to be flounderin' in this here country but it ain't for me to wonder why. This here hub-a-rivers throws up some strange pickin's. But three fresh-faced young'uns like yourselves gotta be the strangest.'

A CRACKED NOTION

The house sways under gentle currents of sand and heaves out creaks of complaint from its joists like a ship at anchor. Inside, it is a jumble of bric-a-brac mostly nailed or tied down – combed, Marshall says, from the dunes. Crates and barrels and engine blocks and truck tyres have been fashioned into such furniture as he needs. Our shadows leap under the light of a swinging oil lamp, and it is snug as we huddle around an iron stove stoked with glowing coals.

Marshall serves the birds with wild onions and herbs from the San Andres Mountains and slabs of corn bread, and it is the finest meal I have tasted in a long while. He feeds choice morsels to an ancient cat named Nugget with broken teeth and torn ears, who resembles a moth-eaten pillow. Nugget listens to the man's constant gabble and gazes at us with a look of such half-lidded contentment that it is hard to imagine how life could be bettered.

'Lazy son-of-a-flea-bitten-molly – he don't even have to round up the rats cos they don't make it onto the land river.'

'You need no perimeter here – it is a Zone doldrums spot?' I ask.

'Nope – Zone here's as active as other places. But, see, its force comes out in the land rivers. If you can live with the flow, ride it some, then you's safe as a bug in a blanket. Been here two summers now, when the stirrin's first started. That's how come it ain't on your map – this here's a new happenin' – spouting up wrecks of towns and riches from the way down below. Kimberlite wells.'

'What's-a-lite?' asks Kelly.

'Kimberlite – molten rock. *Deep*. Like three hundred mile. Satan's forge. Loaded up with minerals. I seen a lava pipe burst up north-a-here sprayin' diamonds big as your fist.'

'No way! Let's see,' asks Kelly.

Marshall shakes his head. 'Let 'em just drift downriver. If I cash in, this place'd be swamped. Dumb-ass rookies fillin' their boots. This here White Sands is *special*. It ain't for gettin' pig-rich off of. Happenin's like this is for a *reason*. Them springs out there start real gentle, just a-tricklin'. But they sure pick up. Mighty tough to cross once they get in their stride. You figured it yet?'

'Is like for guarding this land. Make hard for riders,' answers Luis. 'Zone keep secrets maybe this way.'

'Makin's of a tracker, son. Zone's gotta keep its borders battened down. See, them land rivers pan out from here north and west and they done split territories up into a score of smaller Zones. Like itty-bitty islands. You can't cross it like you used to. Hell, no one can even chart them all cos they changin' course when you ain't expectin'. Man, you don't wanna be hunkered down on your ass when that happens – it'll chew a damn forest into sawdust quicker'n you can run for your worthless life. Well, nuff-a my ramblin' on. I can see you ain't no tourists. Figure you gotta be here on some kinda mission if you're in this deep.'

He waits while Nugget watches us through green-gold eyes that are melting with pleasure. And it is clear he will wait all day for an answer if he has to.

So I begin to tell him all that we have been through so far. He nods and sighs, and his face darkens when I relate the shooting of Marfa's sheriff.

'Mighty grieved to hear that. He's a true officer of the law. I knowed Samuel since he took on the badge. That town don't deserve him. Still, he's the toughest man I ever met – you don't escape the grave but he ain't one to tip into it lightly neither.'

The rest of the tale he listens to tight-lipped, just stroking Nugget behind the ear 'til the room throbs with the sound of pampered purring. The deluge of fish, the

Visitor in Brokeoff, succumbing to the Zone sleep, Carlsbad and the Visitors hiding there, the Mavis Pilgrim, Gallop's story about Yiska, the whereabouts of my pa's grave, the fate of this world that hangs in the balance.

'Last I heard, Yiska was crazy,' says Marshall. 'Zone does that sometimes, breaks a man. Even a tracker, and Yiska was one of the best.'

He sits thinking for a long time, unpicking Nugget's claws from his clothes. He pours us a measure of liquor each and replenishes the stove.

'Spied a big party two days back. They was movin' real fast. Maybe fifteen riders. They went north 'cross the middle of the Sands. Lucky for me or they'd-a seen my set-up here, I guess, but they looked like they'd never-a stopped for no one. Only could be Jethro's boys – no other outfit as big as that these parts.'

'They split,' I reason. 'Some staying for the Mavis, some riding straight to Canyon de Chelly.'

'Maybe they reckoned they don't need the clue we got from the Mavis,' adds Kelly. 'Like all they gotta do is dig up every grave there.'

'Two days ahead,' mutters Luis.

I sigh. 'It can't be helped. At least we know something about the destination that they do not.'

'True,' agrees Marshall. 'And they'd be waylaid by Zone troubles just the same. Two days ain't no disaster.'

'We ain't gonna catch them,' says Kelly. 'Even if we rode day and night. We're all in as it is. How far to Canyon de Chelly?'

Marshall traces a route out on my map. 'Three fifty,

four hundred mile, but you might as well double that in the Zone for all them extra scrapes comin' at you. Well, from here least you ain't got land rivers to cross to get to Spider Rock – 'less you get a real shake-up of the currents. There's a mighty one runs across mesa country, Lost Woman Crater and them places. I followed its banks up as far as Church Rock three month back, but I never went further north cos that's Navajo territory and they sure don't take kindly to intruders.'

I down my liquor. It has the fortifying taste of oak and fire, and it seems to bolster the wild thought I have been entertaining for some time.

'What about if we go *on* the land river itself? We will make up the miles then, for the current will be with us.'

Devon Marshall stares at me, eyebrows climbing up to his cap. Then he erupts into laughter. For a few minutes he cannot speak without collapsing into new gales.

'I met your daddy just after Visitation,' he manages at last. 'Yep, I met the great Virgil Bridgwater when he was the only man to make it to the Pacific and back in one piece. And he told me you had to break the rules if you wanna be a tracker. Craziest damn wanderer I ever shared a whiskey with. 'Til I shared one with you – his daughter! Navigate a land river. Well, god damn if that ain't *the* most cracked notion I ever heard.'

When he has finished drying his eyes, and no further outbursts seem imminent, I tell him. 'Sir, I mean what I say. Tell me how it might be done.'

RAPIDS

Marshall refuses to set off until we have rested. He warns that there will be precious little opportunity for sleep on the land river and beckons us to lie down on a mattress by the wood stove. We three cosy into position, top and tail like sardines in a tin. Luis lies in the middle and makes a show of suffocating from the combined fumes of my feet and Kelly's.

'Yeah, well it stinks like a saloon chunder-bucket up here, buddy,' Kelly says. 'Gonna have to amputate real soon. Bury these puppies in a concrete bunker for a thousand years.'

Luis raises his eyes at me, and again the look strays into something else. I want to meet it, his unwavering gaze, but I don't know how so I turn away and feign exhaustion. On the other side of Luis's blistered feet, Kelly sighs with disappointment, exasperation almost. At these quiet moments, I feel off-balance – another conversation without words leaves me none the wiser.

I feel too keyed up to sleep, my mind running wild with visions of the journey ahead. But the gentle lifting of the sand currents beneath Marshall's house and the glow from the stove send me into deepest slumber.

I wake with a sick start, suddenly worried that I've let my guard down in the Zone, but all is as before. Creaking complaints issue from the house timbers. Nugget has wedged himself between Luis and me – an urgent throb of bliss rises from his bellows-bag body.

Kelly is awake – I watch her for a while as she leans against a porch post outside, gazing at the motionless sun.

I extricate myself from the blankets, taking care not to disturb boy or cat, and join her.

She nods at me, but we don't speak for some while.

'Can't sleep?' I ask at last.

She begins to answer but then cuts herself short. The sand makes a susurrating sound as it sweeps round the piles of the landing stage. Our three horses jostle on the planks, catching their balance as they doze. Marshall's mule has gone.

'Where is he?'

Kelly nods west towards the San Andres Mountains. 'Went to set up a perimeter. Easier to keep watch up there he said. Wants to take stock of the Zone before we set off.'

It is the quiet hour that puts this awkwardness between us, I think. Something about this lonely place, this source of land rivers, that makes us turn inwards. I leave her to her thoughts, but she takes my sleeve.

'Do you think we'll make it, Megan?' There is no imploring tone – she just asks it straight.

'Maybe. It's a miracle we've made it this far. But . . . we . . .' I struggle to explain it, this conviction that I have.

'We are strong.' She finishes it for me. 'Together. The three of us.' She lets out a little laugh. 'The Bridgwater Posse.'

'It is true. Trackers generally move solo. They are loath to trust the judgment of others.'

I think of every occasion where we have needed to rely on each other. And if we were not three . . . Then we would have failed. Lost, split asunder.

'The three of us,' she says again.

It gives my heart a jolt to hear the wistful tone in her voice – that she might have designs to break that bond somehow.

But she says simply, 'I'll be alone when this is done.'

'What?'

'If we make it, I mean. My family all gone. It won't be the same no more, us.'

'What talk is that?'

She captures my gaze then, her hair caught in the wind like a golden streamer. 'I dream about them, Megan. My folks. I always was the kid sister – holding my own, ton of cousins, uncles, aunties, big ol' family getting on my nerves sometimes. But they ain't coming back.'

'You've got us now,' I tell her, meaning it, not just as comfort, but as fact.

'You got Luis,' she murmurs. 'I ain't getting in the way. Three works now but . . .'

'It . . . It's not like that,' I stammer, feeling the blood rush to my face.

She looks at me askance. 'What are you two like?'

'What?'

She pauses, trying to fathom me. 'If you don't know what's as plain as potato pie, then I ain't telling you.'

I'm adrift in this exchange. It worries at me – a ridiculous feeling that they have secrets.

There must be a hard frown on my face, for she says, 'Jesus, Megan. You could try talking to him. That's what the female of the species does best, right?'

A charge of hope laced with jealousy barrels through my chest.

'What's he said to you?' I am unable to remove the last edge of accusation from my voice.

'Hey, I ain't doing this go-between bull. You're on your own.' A little laugh of disbelief, but not unkind.

I block her as she makes to go inside. She raises her eyes to the heavens, and checks past me, to ensure we are not overheard.

'Slow down, sister,' she says softly. 'He ain't said nothing. He don't need to.'

She spruces my collar, all breezy now. And I know behind me Luis is awake.

Her smile is warm, and it is as though she tries the quip

for size, wondering if she can still be the old Kelly, after everything she has been through. She wrinkles her nose at the jacket she bought in Brokeoff not much more than a day ago. 'First I get half the fishing grounds of the Gulf of Mexico dumped on my ass, then I'm target practice for every flying critter in the Midwest! You'd think they was saving it up for me, the way I got it on every square inch. Like how much restroom action can you squeeze out of a bat anyways?'

She reaches in to smell me, holding my eye all the way.

'Phew – you ain't been spared the eau de bat neither. What next do ya reckon? Piss of polecats? I tell you, this ol' Zone is a bummer. I wanna wake up in the Big Rock Candy Mountains, you know, where the hens lay soft-boiled eggs, lemonade springs, all that.'

There is no time for deciphering feelings, mine or anyone else's. Marshall returns soon and we leave his floating house, once more entering the currents of White Sands. The old tracker is highly adept at leading his mule through the drifts. He wades and steers through eddies I see too late, but after an hour of fighting for balance I learn to ride the forces that churn through this place.

Spokes of gleaming sand wend out from the dunes in different directions, and without Marshall's skill, we could have ended up on any one of them. But as the flow picks up on our chosen path northwards, the other land rivers disappear from view. The sand peters out or is churned into a mix of other soils, and the horses shrug out of the shallows onto stronger ground, albeit faster moving. First the fixed peaks of the San Andres Mountains then the Oscura Ridge pass by as we progress. The way the solid banks fall behind, it is like riding Cisco at top clip even though his true pace is a trot. It is unerringly strange to pick a path across a desert in perpetual motion. Fissures are liable to open up at any time as the dirt rolls over itself, tumbling through broken country being made anew. A fine amber cloud of dust rises from these stirrings. Stones slide and are swallowed. Boulders jiggle in their mountings, trembling like ancient heads. But strangest of all is the noise – a deep-in-the-earth grumbling, punctuated by the crack of rock beds long undisturbed, and riding over it all, the rush and rattle of shale, as if the hand of God is panning for gold.

I'm sure the horses would lose their wits but for the ever-present challenge to find sure footing. It takes their minds over, leaving no room for fear. I, too, am absorbed in the task of remaining upright – trying to follow Marshall's mule as it picks its route, nimble as a mountain goat, up and over undulations in the terrain.

We are all sick, except Marshall who must be used to the unnatural motion of land-as-water. The nausea passes, though the unsettling sense that we are in the grip of a drug-induced hallucination does not. In places, I briefly spot the carcasses of small animals, perhaps gophers or rabbits, though it is hard to tell from their formless pelts, crushed no doubt in their burrows. They slither underground or are washed over the shale to the banks.

I shout to Marshall, 'The river has changed course recently?'

He holds back so I'm level with him. 'Yes, Ma'am. It ain't kept in check by the landscape around, the way a real river is. It'll switch back at a moment's notice. But, see.' He points ahead where the course bends further west. 'It meanders some, and it can snap into a new turn, but the broad course is the same. This'un runs up right through old Albuquerque, then hangs west roughly where Route 66 used to be. Brings us within a spit of Navajo country.'

'Where does it end up?'

'Hell, your guess good as mine. Them land rivers carving up the whole northern Zone, but I figure they run outta juice when they hit the Deadline border. Our one probably backs up into the biggest pile-a-dirt in Alaska. Either that or it's chucking out a spur to the noon-waters of the Pacific someplace.'

He barks at me to concentrate on the ground swells at Cisco's hooves. 'Gotta keep one eye on close quarters, Megan! Keep him dancing some or he can get real bogged down in a flash. It's gonna get hairy for the horses somewhere down the line – that's guaranteed. Gotta be ready to bail out if we have to.'

Then, just when I'm thinking the pace of the river will only increase with each mile, the roar abates and we enter a dreamy stretch. The flow dissipates into sluggish dust and gravel, a kind of doldrums. But it is still faster than ordinary riding and we make steady progress. In my head I mark off the journey – Cerro de la Campaña (Hill of the Bell), La Cebolla (The Onion), Sierra de la Cruz. We bank close to the banded rock face of Mesa de la Redonda where the rubble has gouged out a new cliff. We can only pray that the overhangs don't shear off and bury us. It is a new landscape forged from Zone power, like watching ranges form over accelerated millennia.

On and on we ride, until at last we reach a kind of spinning rock plate. It pitches up out of the depths like an enormous raft. It is several hundred metres wide and perhaps twice as long. Marshall gathers us in as we tip and lurch. The sound of boulders being pulverised over the edge is as loud as cannon-fire.

He passes round a water bottle. 'We rest up here for a bit, I reckon. But stay sharp. This baby ain't gonna last five minutes we hit rapids. We break for the bank if things is gettin' rough, you hear me?'

'You telling me this ain't rough already?' Kelly says. Then she is violently sick over the last clean patch of her poncho.

'Stay in the saddle,' says Marshall, unfazed.

We huddle together on the island as it drifts ever northward, sometimes faster, sometimes slower. The nameless land river plots a course between the Rio Bravo and the East Mountains. At times the dust is so thick, it makes a pale disc of the sun and we pull our neckerchiefs over our mouths.

Through a break in the choking cloud, I fancy that I see buildings ahead – the outskirts of Albuquerque. We have covered an astonishing distance – one hundred and thirty-odd miles in just eight hours.

Just as my head is full of figures and routes and remembered fragments of map, a tremendous crack deafens me in one ear.

'Capsize!' yells Marshall.

The slab spills me into a skidding slope. Our island has split in two, no, four . . .

Cisco scrambles backwards, trying not to tip into a gallop.

Beside me Marshall's mule slithers onto its flank, losing purchase as the angle leans practically upright. Marshall half runs, half tumbles, trying to reach it.

And below us, in seething slides of smashed rock, the land river descends into rapids.

RODEO WIPEOUT

Shelves of rock concertina before my eyes. Slabs disappear in a volley of cracks. Cisco teeters above a shadow in the earth. It widens, spilling lumps of stone over the edge, and for a moment we are poised.

He must jump, though the far side is leaning away.

And far, far below I glimpse fires – fleeting traces of molten orange.

I clasp his neck, knowing the leap is too far, and we hang there mid-stride above the chasm.

It ripples, and convulses, and . . . shuts. A thunderous boom of closing earth engulfs us. We flee but so does the land – in toppling waves and leaning towers. A storm of grit blinds me, and when I open my eyes again, I am on a crest of shale, buoyed up somehow by forces from below.

Marshall is no more than twenty metres to one side of me, clinging to his mule, yelling Lord knows what. I wrench around in the saddle.

And see Kelly. She ducks as two gigantic boulders clash above her head then she brings her horse bursting through an updraught of dirt.

I scan wildly for Luis. But he is nowhere. The fixed bank seems so close – I can see trees, their roots exposed, their branches dangling down to the torrent.

Marshall screams my name.

And then it is all wrong – my weight. My legs fly up past Cisco's ears . . . Head whipping back. Reins snapping taut . . .

The sun. Through a hole in rock. Like a window. And a man standing there, draped in a poncho, his back to me. He waits patiently as a sentinel, shimmers in the heat and is gone.

The sun. It moves. A streak of burn. Fast. Slow. Fast. Ground close. It stopped. Did it stop?

My face is pushed against the peaks of mountains, jagged and dry. My face . . . must . . . be . . . huge. Like the sun, that moves. It cannot move. It moves above me, though my eyes are slung on stalks that hang from the sky. So how can I see it move? MOVE. Move. The mountain slopes are so close they are blurred. Blur-red. Blur. Red.

And red rivers run down those valleys. They trickle, stop, start, trickle – pushing like giant drips in the dust.

Noise I can *see*.

Light I can *hear*.

All is wrong. In Wronglands.

The noise I see comes over the horizon. Which is close. Just another line. Like my lashes which move. MOVE. Move. Giddy-up . . . Me-egg-and-me. Meg-and. Meg . . .

'Megan, can you move?'

'Wha-t?'

'Can you move?' Urgent voice. Someone I know.

There is another noise. Judder-thunder. And these tiny-massive mountains that press my face are . . . moving.

'. . . you move? We . . .' Something, something.

I feel broken. I am lying sideways. Recovery position? The ground stretches away like the skin of a drum and upon it bounce stones – billions of them, thrumming and jostling and clacking.

Somewhere in my head I build back. Pa. Zone. Land river.

I crawl, find my legs, my arms. My head is wet with blood. Someone is trying to dab it all away. Kelly. It is Kelly. I'm so grateful to remember her name I nearly start laughing.

'Jesus, that was the greatest rodeo wipeout I've ever seen,' she says.

I look through strands of my hair, claggy with blood. A horse shifts about next to us. Appaloosa. It jerks at a rope, but it's tied to the trunk of a fallen tree. The tree scrapes and flails at the ground, branches half-submerged. Like it's trying to escape, too.

I cast about. There are things missing – people and things.

I stagger onto my hands and knees. 'Cisco! Luis!'

'Hey, take it easy . . .'

'WHERE are they?'

'You got thrown. But Cisco made it. And Marshall.'

'Made it where? WHERE?' I scramble to my feet and drop again as the blood roars into my head.

'To the bank. I saw him lead Cisco out. Poor horse went stir-crazy. Marshall had a job keeping him. But a horse don't buck like that if he's injured.'

I scan all about, but I can't see more than twenty metres before everything goes murky with dust. The land river courses along, but the rapids have passed – it is smooth. Ahead lies the sunset – we are heading due west.

'Luis?' I don't remember seeing him at all after our island-raft disintegrated.

Kelly doesn't answer straightaway. She reaches down to cup my face in her hands. 'I don't know. I didn't see him . . .'

'What?' If I refuse those words they will cease to be. Won't they?

'He's a good rider, Megan.'

We have to go find them. I realise I haven't spoken. My tongue is as dry as leather. 'We have to go find them.'

'Megan, that was two hours ago.'

I stare at her. Her lip is split and her teeth are swabbed with blood. Clods of earth dangle from her hair.

She is a troglodyte.

'Two hours. But . . .'

'You've been out cold. I thought you was dead. Guess you shoulda been, the way you came off Cisco . . .'

'Why didn't you get us to the bank? Two hours ago?'

'Hey!' She backs away from me in sudden disgust. 'You were down, Megan! You don't move someone who's out! Case your back's busted.'

Now I'm angry too. 'So? You can't call an ambulance out here! If my back's broken I'm done for anyway!'

'Getting off makes about as much sense as staying on! Luis could still be on it for all we know, ahead of us, behind us. Goddamn crazy conveyor belt to hell!'

She's right. The rapids just scattered us. There is no simple course of action. My temper blows out. And all I'm left with is a soul sick with worry. My friend. My beloved horse. Lost.

Awful snatches of the land rapids jump to my head. Boulders battering into each other, into dust. I think about how I will not see them again – my horse beset with exhaustion, roaming until he drops. And Luis . . . Luis taken into the earth. I think of the porch at Marshall's house – my last chance to say to him how I feel, how I *really* feel. Gone now. For ever. I feel panic. The Zone's worst danger. It threatens to overwhelm me. A silent, screaming panic – and if I give way to it, if I let it in, there will be no respite. It will undo me.

As three we were strong. Now?

I watch threads of boiling brass run onto the clouds. A sunset that never moves but always changes.

Kelly has her back to me. She is trying not to cry. I watch her overcome it, shaking out the sobs before they can rise to her throat.

'I am sorry,' I say at last. 'Thank you for staying with me.'

She turns and nods, not trusting her voice.

'Do you know where we are?' I ask.

She sends me a half-smile at the futility of the question. Where is anything when the very land itself is on the move?

'Albuquerque was two hours back. That's all I know. What's left of it. Looked like ten twisters went through it.'

And as if to underline the madness of this country, a building emerges from the dusty gloom behind us. It grinds by on a faster current, set at a sharp angle. It is a church – two adobe bell towers slowly separating under the strain. The dull clanging of the one remaining bell passes into the west.

I lean against the fallen tree and try to soothe the Appaloosa – nonsense things I would say to Cisco if he were here. Kelly joins me and together we watch the scenery change. We share the last of her whiskey.

Hours slip by. Kelly dozes, her head thudding gently against my shoulder.

I gaze at the land, hoping for a sign, something to tell me we are close. And as bats give way to swallows, I spot one – a hole in a cliff of russet sandstone. For the briefest of moments I fancy I see a figure standing at the base of the O-shape. A trick in the light? The hole is filled with light like a sun with the red rock as sky. Another fixed sunset. I have never been here, but I know this place. It is a story of the Zone told to me by Pa many times – a premonition of Visitation Day or so the legend goes. Window Rock – sacred to the Navajo.

It is a new day, and we are here at last. The gateway to Canyon de Chelly.

BURIAL GROUNDS

We walk the Appaloosa, to keep him fresh. It is unlikely that we will be welcome in this place – Marshall warned of hostile Navajo, although they are not the only tribe to have returned here. Hopi and Pueblo and Zuni peoples revere the canyon – the ancient home of their ancestors. But the Zone does not respect ownership claims. People of any kind are only tolerated here if they can read the vagaries of Zone forces.

For ten miles or so, we move north, watching on all sides for signs of a threat. Away from the noise and dust of the land river, a profound quiet descends about us. We pass by Navajo farms – barns and trailer homes in advanced states of collapse. Budget supermarkets, flatbed trucks, chain-link fences, propane cylinders – all the mundane debris of a civilisation strewn to the wind.

A feral hound follows us for a mile, whining for food but not brave enough to beg closer. Just as well, as Kelly announces to me that she's hungry enough to eat the mutt raw. She has 'barfed her load on that wilderness travelator' and what little provisions we had were lost from the horse.

The hound leaves us as we enter a southern spur of the canyon proper. It feels like an ill omen that, starving as it is, the dog refuses to follow.

Sounds echo between the rising walls, trapped and amplified – the snorting of the Appaloosa, a strident crow, the swish of swallow tails. We trudge through the soft powder sand of the canyon floor beneath the boughs of olive trees draped in shadow. Above us on the eastern rim, the sun picks out a stripe of bright tan rock, and buzzards lazily patrolling the overlooks. Crouching under the overhangs of cliffs are the ruins of ancient Pueblo homes. I half expect furious tribespeople to charge us from these vantage points, but the canyon is empty.

At the river, we water the horse and take a wash. All the whorls and crinkles of the rock, the iron-grey streaks, the ribbons and crevices and crags – they surround us in the melting forms of a dream. It is a beautiful place, but I feel vulnerable. If we were to be ambushed now, there would be no escape.

Crickets catapult into our clothes like puny sprung

traps. We try to catch them for a snack, but they're too wily.

My Zone quivers are ambiguous. I feel the menace of the place, its melancholy. But also our progress into the deeps of the canyon has become hypnotic.

We aim for the roar of a faster-flowing river and come out of our smaller spur into the majesty of the main canyon.

Kelly grabs my arm. There, at the junction of buttes and winding trails, stand two mighty pillars. Sisters of sandstone. Spider Rock. The split between them runs as narrow and sheer as a cleaver strike. Only the head of the taller tower, two hundred metres or so above us, is dipped in sunshine.

I had held a thought, rarely visited these last hours for fear of jinxing it, that Luis might be here. And Cisco. And Marshall. But the place is empty.

My heart begins to hammer as we skirt the base of the rocks in search of the cemetery. Here I will either hope or despair. The graves run down one shallow and broken slope. There are literally hundreds of them. Why are they here? A battle? A massacre?

We split up, scanning the crosses and markers, slowly at first. But the search becomes feverish for me. There are makeshift crosses fashioned from worm-ridden coffin timbers. There are faded photos in plastic wrappers, and epitaphs scratched into slates, and cairns and twig dolls and shredded bunting. Dearly beloved, sorely missed, rest in peace. Names and years and signs – a litany for the dead. It all whips by in a blur, until at last, under the canopy of a cottonwood, I come to the grave I have been dreading.

One weathered plank is planted at the head of the mound. The writing runs sideways – burnt into the wood with a hot knife by the looks of it. The spelling is wrong. 'Vergil Bridge-Water.' Which makes me fear that he is indeed laid to rest here. A companion has carved his name for posterity – perhaps the tracker Yiska.

Kelly stands beside me and takes my hand. 'Do you want me to do the digging?' she asks.

'I have to see, Kelly.'

We lay aside the rocks that cover the grave and scrape at the dirt, first with our bare hands, then with the plank that bears my father's name. The dry ground is crumbly, easy to shift, and after a few minutes my hand knocks against wood. The coffin is rudimentary – pilfered from other graves. I kneel before it, knowing that whatever it contains has been here since long before this day. My prayers, such as they are, have already been answered or ignored. All that remains is for me to find out which.

I close my eyes and I lever back the lid. In my mind, I see the stiff, flattened shape of a dead man in a coat . . .

The gasp from Kelly makes me look.

And the blood beats in my head.

There are no bones. No remains at all. For several wild seconds I cannot make sense of what it *does* contain.

Kelly jumps into the grave and pulls it out: it is a bundle wrapped in a threadbare Old Glory flag. She unfurls its stars and stripes to the breeze. Inside is a knife made of polished obsidian with an antler handle and a pair of moccasins decorated with white shells.

'Is this a joke?' says Kelly.

'No,' comes a voice from behind us. 'Not a joke. A challenge.'

I draw my gun.

He stands unconcerned – a tall Native American draped in a wool blanket, barefoot. Polished stones hang from his neck. Around his head, a ragged red band. He seems disappointed by what he sees.

'The Zone should have sent three.'

'Yeah, well it's just us two right now,' starts Kelly.

He ignores her, addressing only me. 'You are Megan Bridgwater.'

'You're Yiska, aren't you?' I say.

The tracker who made the map, that marks the clues, that led us here.

'Great,' says Kelly, taking a step towards him. 'So, you can start off by telling us what's the big idea scaring my friend half outta her mind spreading lies about her daddy being dead.'

He holds out his hand to stop her from advancing. Kelly staggers back. There is a gaping hole in Yiska's palm – something inside the wound moves. A nest of blue worms.

'Come no closer. It seeks a more willing host than I.'

'Shoot, Megan! Visitor!'

I stare at the man's eyes – they are grey with the onset of cataract, impenetrable, like two riverbed pebbles.

'Not Visitor. Navajo. I resist. This body is a battle-ground. I will die before it takes me.'

'What do you know of my pa?' I demand. 'Is he alive or dead?'

'Alive. Spirit guide for you on this journey. He is held by *her* in the Valley of the Rocks.'

'Her?'

'She who spawns this plague. We thought her a goddess – the White Shell Woman. Wife of the moon. Mother of the Navajo people. We prayed that she would come to deliver back our lands. Our songs brought her. But she broke the moon, tamed the sun, she is a blight on the Earth.'

'Where's the Valley of the Rocks?'

'The heart of the Zone. *She* waits for you. You have a *choice* to make. Go to her where the rock splits the sky. You must resist, as I have done.' He closes a fist around the worms that infect him.

'Hey,' says Kelly. 'Enough with the riddles, OK?'

He shuts his eyes tight as if fighting a great pain.

The arrow comes from behind us. I hear it before I see it thud into Yiska's chest. It is tipped with flame that makes short work of his blanket. And in an instant he is ablaze. He sways, a grimace of dead-eyed shock on his face. Then he falls into the dust.

LAST WORDS

There are cries and the drumming of hooves behind me, but I do not turn. I snatch the poncho from Kelly's shoulders. Yiska holds the secret of this grave. Without it I fear I will never find my father. I rush to him with the poncho to staunch the flames on his chest.

Yiska barely moves. I think he must be dead already but as I draw back the poncho, I see him blink out of the ruins of his face.

I force myself not to scream. 'Where is the Valley of Rocks?'

His flesh is marbled red. It leaks into the dust. His eyes

wander to the sky behind me, beseeching, already fading. I try to arrest that gaze, to bring it to Earth.

'Where?'

The pupils open, close, open. But they rest on me at last.

'Choose,' he whispers. 'You must choose.'

'What do you mean? I don't know how.'

'Face her.'

'Yiska!'

I lose him again. Deliverance beckons. A scuff of boots on shale draws closer.

'In the grave . . . your choice.'

'The moccasins? I don't understand. Stay with me.'

'Visitors are . . . weak. She *needs* you.'

Kelly barks at someone to unhand her. Her throttled rage is met with laughter. No, not laughter – something like a rendition of it, mirthless. The leisurely draw of gun from holster has a distinctive creak to it. Yiska recognises it too, greets it with a pained smile. Shadows fall upon us. Will I hear it when it comes – the gunshot? But this one is not for me. The barrel glances my cheek on its way to rest point blank beside the arrow shaft. There is a calm about the killing, the way a broken horse is put down. Yiska blinks but the boom leaves him half-lidded. I feel the jolt as a life is taken.

'There,' comes a voice from behind. 'How easy a soul departs. Easier than its arrival. Wouldn't you say, Megan Bridgwater?'

I turn, but sunlight on the far canyon rim flares behind the figure like the corona of an eclipse. I see only shadow, until the head bows closer.

It's a reflex, my scrambling away, one that I'm power-less to resist. I am a child in the throes of a nightmare, such is the horror that faces me.

'Do not be afraid. It comes to us all. Even the late Jethro Wells.'

There are no lips to make these words – they issue from a place deep inside the animated cadaver before me.

A greenish hand gestures at the face – at the gobbets of meat and glistening cheekbones, at the grin of Death himself. 'Poor Jethro. Son of a truck driver and a mail clerk. More famous dead than alive. I should get a new host, but I'm attached to this one. Helps no end with the terrifying I must do. Any self-respecting outlaw would agree.'

The teeth nudge, loose in their withered gums. The eyeballs are awful to behold. They flicker with tiny topaz fires – naked in an expression of permanent alarm. A bulge from one socket has the impossible aspect of a tear, but it is just a maggot worming free. A flurry of others follow, wriggling into the light. The Visitor-in-chief hobbles closer with a halting gait, sloughing bits of flesh as it strides. Here and there through rents in the clothing, at the elbows, at the knees, I see glimpses of blue fibre – strands of the alien body within.

An abattoir stench washes over me. 'What a merry, merry dance you have led us. But it ends here. Your mistake, should you care to know, was to leave that sorry survivor of the Mavis Pilgrim.'

For the first time, I am aware of other figures closing in

around me – outlaws and tribesmen. The corpse of Jethro Wells turns to them, as awkward as a broken marionette. 'Hogart was the name he gave us, I believe. Before he died. He overheard every word of your plans. You should have dispatched him when you had the chance.'

Out of the corner of my eye, I spot Kelly – trussed up but struggling. Navajo warriors, or their stolen forms, watch over her.

'No word from the great tracker's daughter?'

The voice has an unearthly tone – pressed out in gusts as though from a punctured barrel organ. Wafts of rot escape with each phrase.

'How convenient, this ready-made grave. How fitting. Look about you. This is where your Zone adventure fails. This is where the hopes of your race die. Your father was indeed cunning – to have hidden away his hard-won secrets. Even more cunning to have laid a trail for you to find them.'

I find a way to my feet. 'Take me to the Valley of the Rocks,' I demand.

The head cocks to one side. 'I shall. But first you must say goodbye to your friend.'

He turns to face Kelly, who starts to struggle.

'Leave her!' I cry. 'Let her go! You are to take me to the Valley of the Rocks now!'

'You command me, mongrel child? My orders are from her. You are to come *alone*.'

As the voice rises in volume, so a flap of skin in Jethro's throat vibrates. He points at Kelly. 'Hang her.'

'No!'

I chase forward to reach Kelly, but strong hands hold me back.

It takes no more than a minute for the Visitors to tie Kelly's hands and bundle her onto a horse.

She watches me and makes a great effort to compose herself. No more struggling. The horse shifts nervously as a noose is slung over the branches of the cemetery cottonwood.

'Not going for the ol' frozen touch of death then?' says Kelly with admirable steadiness.

'You would prefer it? Your body preserved for posterity?' replies the Jethro Visitor.

'If you're giving me a choice I'll go for with-my-boots-on-aged-ninety-five.'

'The manner of your death is fitting. Not that you shall ever see it now, but we have a noose around this entire world, a stranglehold that will not now be broken.'

'Got any ideas?' Kelly says to me, almost in passing.

I watch her in a daze. Words have abandoned me.

In desperation, I turn to the impassive faces of the tribesmen around us. The way they are dressed for war, in feathers and paint and wolf skins, makes me hope that they are perhaps human. Why would they honour these traditions otherwise? If they are in thrall to Jethro, maybe they can be turned. Perhaps they can resist like Yiska. But now they are near enough for me to see their eyes – copper bright and dead as coins.

'There was a boy also,' one of the outlaws says. It is the ugly one we have brushed with before – in Brokeoff and at the Mavis.

Jethro whirls and shoots. The outlaw staggers back from the blast.

'Yes, a boy.' One, two, three more shots. 'Who should be in a shallow grave.'

The others cringe from the murder in a way that could never be described as human. They submit to their demented lord, shaking in weird convulsions. The slaughtered one lies in the dirt and its wounds are so deep that its strands spill out like a disturbed nest of snakes.

Jethro stumps back to us. 'Where is the boy?'

Kelly and I both stare at each other.

'No matter. If he is alive I will leave others to wait for him. Any last words?'

'Yeah,' says Kelly. 'But not for you.'

I expect gallows humour. But her voice is quiet, just for me. She says a prayer for our souls and those of her family. She names each Tillman – a roll-call that will never be answered. And then she sings. Her clear voice reverberates across the lonely slope – a country song about a woman who waits for her lover to return from the Civil War. What surprises me is the effect it has on our captors – they stare at her, transfixed almost. Perhaps music means something to them.

I think she is trying to appeal to them, to unlock a crumb of pity. But I have seen into their visions. I know they are ruthless in their pursuit to conquer. Each verse turns out another chapter in the woman's ongoing misfortune – it is a lengthy tale.

And then I realise.

I turn to follow Kelly's fixed line of sight, and in the

distance, out of canyon shadow I spy a trail of dust. A lone rider.

Kelly finds another line, and another. There are repeats, and a few improvisations that almost work, but not quite.

Jethro raises one decomposing arm. 'Enough!'

I snatch a glance behind me. For a few moments, the rider disappears below the brow of a dip.

Where the thought sparks from I cannot say. I recall the Visitor at Brokeoff, the one who has just been killed. *Your mother! That witch! We should have hunted her down sooner.*

'My mother,' I say. 'Why did you despise her?'

Jethro turns from Kelly. He drags so close to me that I can see flies feasting on old sores.

The Navajo's words return to me. *The Visitors . . . are weak.*

'She resisted, didn't she?' I whisper. 'Like Yiska.'

Jethro nods, dislodging one of the vertebrae, so that the head cricks to one side.

Even as I say these words, the meaning of them is slow to crystallise. And yet I feel I have always known.

You don't know, do you?

That witch!

Mongrel child . . .

My mother was a Visitor.

Suddenly the rider emerges. He rides at full tilt, arm aloft, brandishing a rifle. My heart leaps at the sight. It is Luis. And I would recognise that horse anywhere. It will be only seconds before we hear their approach. This

234

desperate charge will come too late, in vain, for what can he do alone against so many?

One of the Navajo braves lets out a cry.

Jethro staggers to the tree and seizes the reins of Kelly's horse.

A shot rings out. Then another. Visitors fall and scatter.

'Kelly!'

Her eyes fix to mine and she takes a mighty breath.

The saddle slides from under her and the noose snaps shut.

'KELLY!'

Jethro throws his dead arm at me, full force. A sodden blow to the teeth.

Squelch of rotten flesh.

The horizon swings before me.

No sound.

Just Cisco tearing into the cemetery. And Luis firing from the hip.

GRAVE GOODS

Chaos unfolds about me. It has the frantic hallmark of a skirmish, but I cannot make out details – only the wrestling motion of dust and bodies. It is happening now, I tell myself, though it appears to recede into distant history.

Pain skewers my jaw. *Isn't that good – pain? Isn't that life?*

I find that I am lying face-up. My whole body is seized by pins and needles. Someone is punching me. No, that is just my breathing. The rasps from my lungs have the scrape of spurs on gravel.

Smells and sounds and light assault me. All at once,

together in a great upheaval – salt-blood-grit-whooping-cough-gun-smoke-blaze.

Luis props me up, though I am as weak as a mewling cub. He lifts me clean off the ground, holds me close. A stream of Spanish prayers spill from his lips, too fast for me to catch. I hear promises to God, as if he is haggling for my life.

'I knew you'd come,' I croak.

From over his shoulder Cisco's huge wet-whiskered muzzle nestles into my face, snorting and searching for my smell.

Luis stands me up gently, hands hovering in case I should keel over. The graveyard is scattered with dead Visitors.

'How?'

'Don't speaking now,' he urges. 'Is Marshall, from there, he shoot.' He points to an escarpment opposite Spider Rock.

'Damn, he's one hell of a shot.' Kelly has acquired the voice of a wheezing saloon regular.

She sways drunkenly toward me, her hands still tied behind her back, the chopped noose swinging from her neck. 'Where's the zombie bad-ass?'

We cast around among the fallen, but Jethro is not one of them.

'Some ride away. Eight, I think. Not together. Some south, some east.'

With a dagger, Luis cuts Kelly's bonds. We stand in an exhausted daze, blinking at each other. As three once more.

Water, sweet water. It tumbles over my face, and I drink it down in great painful gulps, watching as Marshall canters over the canyon floor from his vantage point. I feel raw and pounded and sick. But my head begins to work. We cannot stay here long. Jethro will regroup for another attack no doubt.

Marshall smiles at me as he dismounts from his mule. 'Sure reckon you two used up more lives than Nugget.' He waves away my thanks.

'If they'da hung Kelly higher with more slack she'da croaked on the first swing. I tried for the rope but you only hit that in the movies I figure. Drew a bead on the leader, reckon I hit him too, but didn't slow him down none.'

'He's already dead,' I mutter.

'Huh?'

I try to explain.

'Musta just clipped the human hide then. Either way we stole a march on them sons of bitches . . .' His voice trails away when he sees Yiska's body.

He takes off his hat, pulls the burnt poncho over Yiska's face and makes the sign of the cross.

I tell them about Yiska; how the Navajo brought Visitation upon the Earth; about the White Shell Woman they thought they'd summoned. I tell them about Yiska's resistance; his last words.

From the excavated grave I retrieve the flag, the moccasins, and the knife.

'What is this?' asks Luis.

'These things represent a choice I must make.'

'You?' Luis frowns at me.

'Something lives at the heart of the Zone. At the Valley of the Rocks. Like a goddess. She holds Pa. She waits for me. I must face her.'

'She wants you?' Luis looks frightened. 'Why?'

How can I tell them what I know? I wipe some blood from my mouth. It is red, just like human blood. But I am not human. Part of me is Visitor. A human father and an abductee mother. My body has not been stolen. It has been *made*.

Should I not feel horror? Instead I feel layers of mystery falling away from me. It makes sense now. Why I am so clueless at matters of the heart. Why I feel the Zone so strongly. Why the Visitors do not revolt me as perhaps they should.

I gaze at my friends. They will not understand, they will not accept, how can they? They have lost their families to Visitation. I remember when we first met Kelly, after Luis threatened her with a gun, they sealed a pact to kill each other should either of them succumb to abduction. The Visitor essence of me would surely repel them.

I weigh the grave goods in my hands. A symbolic choice? Knife or white shell moccasins? What does it mean?

'I must go to the Valley of the Rocks.'

'We,' corrects Luis. '*We* must go.'

'Yeah, if we knew where the hell it was,' says Kelly.

'Valley of the Rocks is the Navajo name for it,' answers Marshall. 'Better known as Monument Valley. It's marked by three sandstone buttes.'

'Where the rock splits the sky,' I murmur.

I stare out west. All this time we have fled Jethro's gang, and all this time I have followed the trail my father left for me. But either way the destination remains the same. Why was it so important for me to come to the heart of the Zone with my three companions, when as a captive of Jethro I would have ended up in the same place?

Only Pa will know. Was I right to trust his messages?

I march over to Cisco, kiss him on the forelock, and yank the saddlebags to the ground. I pull out cans of pinto beans and toss them to my weary companions. Kelly catches hers but looks confused as I pull the ring-top on mine and glug it all down with its honey sauce.

'Strip down your packs, anything that might slow us down,' I say between syrupy mouthfuls. 'We take water and guns. That's it. Jethro knows Monument Valley's where we're going. So we fuel up now and move out. You too, Marshall. You'll have to take one of the Visitor horses – your mule is too slow.'

Marshall shakes his head and chuckles. 'Well, Ma'am, I appreciate you stepping up. And it's a good plan'n'all. Can't fault it much anyhow.'

I wipe the juice from my face. 'But?'

'But I ain't going. I'm staying here. Rear-guard action . . .'

Luis starts to complain but Marshall holds his hand up. 'Now, listen up. Jethro's coming back here. Has to. See if you made it or not. And when he does ol' Marshall's gonna be waiting.' He pats his rifle. 'Do more damage with this in an ambush than out in the open. Stands to reason. I'm just surplus to requirements. Best thing I can do is watch your back.'

We stand in silence for a moment. Luis hangs his head. It is the tone in Marshall's voice that betrays the truth we all know but won't speak of. It is a last-stand situation. He cannot hope to hold them all off from afar – he must wait until they are close to have any chance.

'Is too many,' says Luis quietly. 'Eight.'

'Well, now I counted seven. Listen, I ain't planning on leaving my mule or Nugget to fend for themselves. You do what you got to. Then we got ourselves a White Sands rendezvous, see?'

Luis says nothing, refuses to meet his eye. Marshall tuts and grumbles and walks over to him. They have some private words in Spanish and embrace. I can only guess at the things they have been through since the land river. Luis mounts up first and starts to ride slowly west, waiting for us to catch him up.

I think there are tears standing in Marshall's eye but he's gruff with us. 'Get gone now. I ain't standing on no ceremony here. Can't shoot straight when things is getting emotional.'

Kelly springs up and gives him a hug he pretends he has no time for. But I see him smile anyway. What man wouldn't? He holds his hand out to me.

'Tracker to tracker,' he says. 'You head west out the canyon, follow the mesas north. Should hit a two-bit place called Kayenta. Cross the river there and you got the road takes you into the Valley. Forty, fifty mile. Tell

Virgil he owes me a drink. Hell, he owes me a whole bottle-a sour-mash. And he can deliver it to the saloon I'm building at White Sands.'

Kelly and I ride in silence after Luis. I keep turning in my saddle and Marshall is there watching us by the shade of the cottonwood. When we are three abreast on the canyon floor I turn again but he has gone.

We keep a brisk pace, turning out of the canyon, through the reservation town of Chinle, and out onto the ochre plains.

We are together but it is a lonely ride. The Zone is oppressive here. Unseen power hangs in every stone, every tree, every spiky outline against the sky.

Wind kicks up. It funnels along the edge of the mesa walls that steer us north. I keep the perimeter for ten miles before I even realise I'm doing it. It has become natural, habitual. I am a tracker of this land at last. The huge squared-off buttresses that enclose us in shadow are rocks no more to me. They are markers steeped in a vast sea of Zone currents, and I feel those currents wash through my skull.

I take soundings. The pages of the Rand McNally have somehow migrated *inside*. Perhaps I have stared at them so many times they are ingrained. Or perhaps, they sit redundant over my thoughts now. Because with each mile north, I feel it – a gathering grip in the very air, so sharp that it practically sings. We are moving to its heart now. The place where the Zone begins and ends.

WHERE THE ROCK
SPLITS THE SKY

The streets of Kayenta are the same as any number of other lost towns of these once united states. Wide strips of empty concrete. A motel painted swimming-pool blue. Traffic lights that swing from curved steel gibbets. The sidewalks and burger stops and convenience stores are relics of a complacent way of being that cannot return, I think, even if people came back. The human race has been shaken from its slumber, snatched to the brink of ruin.

Normal is no more.

A herd of wild mustangs linger by the bridge. They shy from us into upstream shallows.

An enormous recreational vehicle stands across both lanes in the middle of the bridge. Black lines of rubber mark the wild braking that brought it to a halt. Its two decks are clad in rustic planking that make it look more like a log cabin on wheels than a vehicle. Nothing has been plundered. It is as it was when its occupants fled – cooler boxes and mountain bikes and fluffy dice. The signs of this unknown panic long since over haunts me with dread. We are so far in-Zone that no one dares to trespass, even to scavenge.

On the far side of the river, we encounter the first of the traps. To me it is apparent – a sinkhole in the road so thick with flies that it's hard to make out what it contains. But as we approach, it is clear the others have not registered it at all. I have to grab Kelly's reins before she rides straight into it. Not even her horse baulks, which puzzles me, until I realise only Cisco among our horses is untouched by the Visitor brand.

'Hey!' snaps Kelly.

'Believe me, there are dangers you cannot sense. Dismount and you may see it.'

Luis jumps back in alarm as soon as his boots touch the ground. 'Jesús! What is it?'

'Last line of defence. This is the core of the Zone.'

The stench is epic but not identifiable – dark, industrial, poisonous. The flies hover but do not settle onto the glinting filth below as if they are intoxicated and repelled in equal measure.

'Should we ditch the Visitor horses?' asks Kelly.

I take a few moments to think it through. My instinct is clear. 'No, it may be a trick to get us to do just that. Just walk them for a while. I should go first.'

'Be my guest. Man, this place is really booby-trapped, huh?'

'I would not think any tracker has reached this point and survived. Except my father.'

Kelly looks at me askance. She perhaps senses that my reading of the Zone has reached another level. I wonder at the secrets I harbour then. She and Luis will surely know before the day is out anyway – what I really am. I tell myself I must concentrate on the perils at hand. But would they even be here with me if they knew?

Several miles further north we come to a top-heavy tower of boulders, again set in the middle of the road. Like the town of Valentine, it denies gravity. The blocks grind against each other, shifting uneasily.

'Who goes first?' asks Luis.

'Wait.' I snap a branch from a dead tree and get ready to cast it. 'Ride when I say. And ride fast!'

As soon as I toss the branch, the tower convulses and the rocks crash down. They agitate in their craters, eroding corners with sudden tremors.

'Now!'

The rocks whirl and blur as we scramble past so that the air is filled with flakes and splinters. At the next bend, I feel we are clear, and as I look back, the boulders have silently reassembled into their tower. If Luis and Kelly had abandoned their horses at the pit, the boulders would have blocked their passage.

It is Kelly who first spots it – a wound in the indigo sky. It emerges as a crooked fracture when we are still perhaps twenty miles from Monument Valley. The fissure dwindles as it rises, disappearing into a hairline as thin as gossamer. *Where the rock splits the sky.*

It is an effort to tear my eyes from it as we progress ever closer. The road bends slightly to the east on the final approach, and when we are close enough to make out the three buttes of Monument Valley, I realise the sky is not wounded at all. It is a solid structure, a kind of tower, that dwarfs the natural rocks, hovering above them, apparently anchored in nothing but roiling air. The base of the structure is so thick it spans the entire area between the three buttes. It spirals as it rises, slanting and sprouting from the central core. At unimaginable altitudes I can make out filigree platforms, frayed buds. The stem courses with electric flashes that light the valley floor.

'What on God's Earth *is* that?' breathes Kelly.

'No wonder the Navajo believed it meant the return of their White Shell Woman.'

'Yeah, pretty much blows away them other monuments.'

Luis hands me the spyglass and points to the platforms. 'Lost towns,' he says simply.

He's right. When I focus the view, I see the uprooted edges of suburbs, drooping highways, the ripples of streets. These are the casualties of abduction, hoarded in the heavens. This is where Kelly came from.

The tower casts a twisting shadow eastwards like a scar, ten miles, twenty miles? Perhaps it only peters out with the curvature of the Earth. I try, and fail, to comprehend its scale. A thing *made of* vertigo. It stands over the land like a monstrous totem, or a tether holding the Earth in a slipknot, and yet its appearance seems as nothing to its *presence*.

This is where the Zone radiates its power. You feel it in strange jumps of the air, moments that seem to judder into reverse as you pass through them. A jackrabbit hurtles over the scrub in crazed leaps. Weird snatches of sound break out of nowhere – rushes of water or forest fire or radio crackles. I swear that, just in a space of a blink, Cisco's mane changes white silver and back again. Soft glows wink at the edge of your vision, but when you chase them down they vanish.

Kelly says, 'You know, just one time, I'd like things to be way-back-when. Like boring. I kinda miss that. Not worrying that a 7-Eleven is gonna explode in my face or something.'

I turn to her, but it's as though her voice has issued from the vacant air because she is riding some way ahead of me. This is how the Zone plays its tricks.

I pick up the pace as we ride ever closer – the plain is so open I feel we are exposed. With the sun at our backs, cantering shadows stretch before us. I spur Cisco into a gallop, perhaps the final one he has strength for. Each stride feels like the last before a cliff edge. There will be no return from this place if I falter. And as we ride, I feel the Zone close around us, as a parting sea thunders back to claim its dominion.

The air over and between the butte summits warps and contracts so that the rocks seem to writhe, as sinuous as bonfire updraughts. I imagine its forces running untrammelled around the circumference of the Earth, under and over the crust, through a mantle of molten rock – the noose that pulls us to a grim fate.

We slow to a trot in close formation as we approach the centre of the valley, moving warily into the shadow of the tether's mouth.

The structure's canopy looms over us, rising into a fathomless hollow. We pick a way between the bruise-coloured tendrils that hang from its underbelly, sometimes reaching the ground in coarse knots.

'Do you reckon it's alive?' asks Kelly. She peers at one of the weird hanging ropes and leans out of her saddle a little to take a sniff.

'Don't touch!' cries Luis, snatching her back.

'Hey, I'm just throwing it out there! You think I wanna touch it?'

Below the very centre of the tether base is the heart of the valley, the place where the monuments stand equidistant from us at the points of a triangle. Before us lies a vast heap of bleached white shells. There are millions of them, of different kinds, banked into a curved beach – urchins and coral pieces, conches and razor clams, shattered and whole. They are dead, but they move – sliding over one another endlessly into new shapes. It is eerily quiet under the tether – not so much as a breeze stirs. Only the shells move – like the insistent scratching of countless buried claws.

Kelly says, 'You know, just one time, I'd like things to just be way-back-when. Like boring . . .'

'I kind of miss that,' I mutter. 'Not worrying that a Seven-Eleven will explode in my face. Or something.'

We both frown at each other. Time has slipped gear. Sometimes-never-always.

I climb down from Cisco and unravel the Old Glory flag. White shell moccasins or obsidian knife? The moccasins are exquisitely made, sewn and shaped for pampered feet. What are they for? What was Pa trying to tell me? Perhaps they are an invitation . . .

Luis calls out, 'Company, Megan!'

Closing in from every direction come riders. Perhaps thousands of them – the dead and shredded flesh of Navajos and bandits. An army of Visitors.

'Maybe too much company,' mutters Kelly. 'S'pose now ain't the time to say I reckon I shoulda gone to Fort Stockton like y'all said.'

The Visitors encircle us completely and dismount.

Jethro emerges from the throng. The corpse tilts into the wind. It shakes its arm violently and fingers scatter to the ground. What emerges from the coat sleeve is an approximation of a human hand made from twisted fibres as thick as tendons. It moves towards me.

'Stop!' cries Luis. He raises his rifle and fires a single round into Jethro's chest.

I grab the barrel of Luis's weapon and point it to the ground. We cannot hope to win a gunfight.

The Visitor stumbles and seems to contemplate this latest wound. The alien fibres retreat. Then the entire requisitioned body of Jethro Wells disintegrates. A new shape tips out of the remains, spilling and massing into a headless thing on five segmented limbs. One of the limbs reaches down to the discarded human remains and spikes Jethro's head. It holds up the skull for me and hinges the jaw as a puppeteer might. I am so horror-struck that, as it scuttles towards me, I am powerless to respond, too scared even to run.

Slits in the Visitor's barrel-shaped body issue a command. 'Fall before the White Shell Woman.'

Yiska talked of the White Shell Woman – Navajo goddess, wife of the moon – but the dead sockets of the Jethro's skull seem to point at *me*. For one awful moment, my mind, my nerve, everything deserts me. I am lost. Even my name holds no meaning.

Kelly stares at the moccasins in my hands. 'Feel free to fill us in here,' she says shakily.

'But I don't know. I mean . . . None of this . . . It doesn't make sense.'

Nothing feels true. I stare at my own fingers, the lines of my palms. My flesh just seems *wrong*. Empty somehow. Waiting for someone to claim it.

Luis takes a step back from me.

Marfa, Carlsbad, Spider Rock – over and over again the moments replay. The cold touch of Visitors, and how I am *like* them. How I just *look* human. From the outside. But what am I *inside*?

All the riders around us dismount and drop to

their knees.

I cannot bear to watch my friends edging away. Only now do I really understand what I'm losing if they should go or die. I have loved them – I see that now. And they have loved me in return. But with every moment that passes unchecked, I become alone.

'I am both,' I say at last.

Kelly's voice is hollow. 'Both what?'

Every fibre of me feels like a lie. I want to run and never stop. I want to scream and never take breath. But I will not escape the truth. I am not a person. I am just the semblance of one.

'My father is human. My mother was Visitor.'

My friends are speechless. Luis drops his rifle. Kelly shakes her head. The look on their faces can only be described as betrayal.

'I did not know. I found out at Spider Rock.'

'You are White Shell Woman?' stutters Luis. He will not meet my eyes.

I think of shells. Only of shells. Husks to be filled with new life.

Luis shouts my name, desperate for an answer. Am I her? Am I White Shell Woman?

'I don't know,' I murmur. 'I don't know.'

A rushing sound fills the air, dry and brittle, like the sound of a million rattlesnakes. The white shell beach rises and collects itself, gathering into an airborne mantle. It coils and dumps itself into new shapes with the momentum of waterfalls. Beautiful strands sprout and loop, delicate as necklaces. Then with the thunder of an entire shoreline breaking, a head made of shells turns to face us.

'No,' says Kelly. '*That* is White Shell Woman.'

TAKER OF WORLDS

The shifting curtain of shells mimics a woman's face. No, not one woman. Many. Each face configures into the next, though the expression remains the same – eyes closed, in meditation or sleep.

The kneeling Visitor army begins to chant – a worship without words to their mother and goddess.

But then a frown convulses across that giant likeness.

The lips do not part but she speaks. A rush of tumbling shells made into a voice without feeling.

Cease.

The Visitor hoard stops chanting and lies on the

253

ground in submission.

You bring the Bridgwater child. But not alone.

Hissing from the shells rises in pitch.

The horses begin to snort and champ. I let go of Cisco's reins. We are on the cusp of something terrible. At least I can save my horse – I picture him joining the wild herd at Kayenta. With a wild cry, I send him packing. He charges free, released at last from this madness. He sparks a stampede as all the other horses break away in different directions.

A low moan rises from the Visitor army.

You are weak.

The transformation from face to tornado happens in a blink. Wind tears at our clothes and hair. The shells howl as they accelerate into a white storm. It arcs over our heads like a giant scorpion back. There's nowhere to run to, nowhere to hide. All we can do is stand and watch.

Visitor screams are lost in a hail of grit. Their bodies are annihilated into pink mist. The slaughter takes less than a minute.

We stand, trembling. Awaiting our fate. But the carnage ends and the stained shells reassemble, the calm face dripping with meat. Nothing remains of her brood but tattered clothes and boots.

She opens her eyes and gazes at me with a horrifying intensity. I am transfixed.

You have come. The Zone is your home. You are strong. The first of a new kind. You bring to the mixed blood of a billion races . . . the blood of the human race. Your young will conquer. Now you will rule for me. This world and others beyond counting will be yours, my child.

I cannot move. Inside she is hollow, filled only with distant golden fire – the fire that drives her to conquer galaxies. I look at the white shell moccasins, shoes for a Navajo queen, and understand at last. Her time has come. Yiska was right – she is weak. I am to succeed her. I am to be the White Shell Woman when she is dead.

Luis and Kelly stumble away from me. I have lost them.

I feel the lure of the Zone. It runs through me. This wild and deadly place I love. It will spread to the ends of the Earth. She promises it will be mine.

I watch my friends. They seem small. They keep their distance but they do not run.

As I stand motionless, the tether's tendrils begin to close around my body, over my legs.

'Megan!' shouts Luis. My name sounds wrong. Like it belongs to someone else now.

He wants me to run. But there is nowhere to run. The tendrils bind me. The Zone is all around us. *She* is both tether and Zone.

Luis makes a step towards me but Kelly hauls him back. They are both crying now. Tears. I remember them in the dark. In the deep dark of Carlsbad. The sweetest pain.

And I remember that I have a choice.

I look up at the white shell face. And I drop the moccasins into the dust.

She sees my mind. That I can resist her. That I choose to be human. That I choose the love of Luis and Kelly –

two mortal, frail beings. That against that, all the power she can bestow on me is nothing. A fury of golden flame spouts from her eyes.

The tendrils quicken about me in loops and knots. More vines drop from the canopy, tumbling and writhing in their hunger to reach me.

If I will not join her, then I will be taken.

Kelly screams and Luis makes a run for it but tentacles snatch their legs from under them.

'Let them go!' I yell.

I brandish the obsidian knife and slash out as the tentacles come for me. My blows are wild, opening up gashes of yellow ooze. I hack and thrust until my hands are slippery with alien blood, *her* blood. But still the tentacles rush in. She could destroy me, rip me limb from limb, but, when it comes, her embrace is almost *forgiving*. As a mother to a wayward daughter. Her flesh coils around my throat. I feel her skin, rough against mine, and thousands of tiny barbs fixing to my pulse.

I sway there for a moment, too stunned to fight, my head thrown back towards the sky. Luis and Kelly wrestle in the air above. A maw opens for them in the canopy. The air ripples with heat and the stench of clotted blood reaches me. I sense the countless lives lost here. This gigantic tether that binds the Earth is the hive where humans and Visitors are joined.

The tentacles take their first draw of my blood. I feel it pump from my throat. A leach-like grip takes hold, hungry for more. But then as my head starts to spin, the blood returns – a sudden tide of warmth. Not just my blood – *hers and mine, blending and changing*. A toxic swirl. Through it I feel her immense age. She is a taker of worlds. But she is *sluggish* now. At the end of her dominion. She needs a successor, she needs my blood, she needs me.

The tentacles flex again. This time the pull on my bloodstream is so deep I feel my heart stutter. Every vessel in my body runs cold. Then the flush of new blood like a release, the breath that saves you from drowning. But this mingling is a kind of death. I know it. It bursts through me – a relentless rush. Like the urge to kill, again and again and again. I have perhaps only seconds before this exchange changes me for ever. I will become the White Shell Woman – her cold spirit will live on through me.

And if I yield to her now, humankind will be swept from the face of this world. The bodies of every last person will be taken to hatch a new race of Visitors.

But I still have a knife. I still have a choice, and it is as clear to me as the forever sunset. Immortality in the shoes of a queen or a fight to the death. It is the choice my pa knew I would have to make.

The tentacles around my throat tense again.

I stare at the White Shell Woman, at her eyes of fire. She waits – calculating, assessing my intent. Do I really have the guts to challenge her?

And I thrust the knife upwards. Straight through the collar of tentacles. Tether sinews snap and fly apart. A great wash of amber liquid spills down my front. My blood and hers. It fizzes on the sand.

For a moment I stand tall – I feel free, strong almost.

257

The hacked tentacles writhe and thump the ground. But then a terrible burning seizes my throat – the pain of all those tiny barbs ripped from the skin. I reach up to stem the flow and blood cascades over my fingers.

A demonic screech fills the air.

And I see it clearly in all those hissing pools of amber leaking into the dust. She cannot survive without me. Without my blood she will die.

I force my gaze upwards. Luis and Kelly dangle at the mouth of the hive – they hang motionless, perhaps too terrified to fight any more. The opening glows with luminous secretions. Inside there are undulating fronds, coralline twists, oxbow folds – all pulsing. They unfurl slowly – the petals of a hideous flower. Stacked up to the sky and beyond, I can see storey upon storey of cells, regular as lizard scales, beating soundlessly. And trapped inside them, the shadowy forms of abductees.

What will become of them? This thought arrives slowly, coming to rest unspoken on my lips.

The largest breath I can take is pitiful. My choice is made. And here comes the price.

It is astonishing how quickly life begins to desert me. Each beat of my heart is so much feebler than the last. And as I gaze through faltering eyes, I see the White Shell Woman. Her face collapses in landslides of white. Above me, fractures run along the great tether walls, opening rents of fire. Detonations race up to the clouds – stays and ties and frames buckling into accelerated collapse.

The knife tumbles from my hand.

Noise retreats on an outgoing tide.

Already my blood runs cold.

I see it as I fall – the tether whiplashing into low banks of cloud. Mile-long sections of it unzip and plummet gracefully westward. Abducted towns puff to Earth in the far distance. It is like watching a divinity make a range of mountains, sowing them into a straight course over the horizon.

Tentacles spill down into giant worm-casts.

My face thuds into the dirt.

More lives than a cat. Not this time.

My breaths are red, they bubble away.

A boy screams over me. I feel his hands at my neck, my face, my lips – searching for a way to staunch the flow. He bellows my name so close I feel his breath on my cheek. I know this boy, but his name escapes me. If I could just remember it, I would live. I picture him in the light of the forge. *De nada*, he says, over and over again. And I have hurt him with my thoughtlessness. But he came with me anyway.

Luis. His name is Luis.

NIGHT

I awake in a cocoon of blankets with only enough strength to open one eye. My throat throbs with a raw pain. A thick dressing covers the wound.

A makeshift camp surrounds me – low-slung tents fashioned from ponchos and branches. Around me, tied horses whinny and jostle. One of them tugs at his rope, straining to reach me. Cisco!

I struggle to sit up. In every direction, men, women and children lie in rows like a vast field hospital. The survivors of abduction. Some joke and chat and cough, propped up on their elbows, or being fed by others more able.

A hundred metres or so away lies the wreckage of the toppled alien tether. People are still emerging from it dazed and stooped, propping each up.

One of them walks slowly towards me – a man. He brushes away offers of help. His long hair and beard are streaked with grey. It takes an age for me to recognise him. Because he is old beyond his years. A castaway stranded in the Zone.

I call out to him. 'Pa?'

He embraces me gently and whispers in my ear. 'Megan. My Megan. I'm so sorry.' He brushes the hair from my eyes.

'Sorry?' Delicious fatigue tugs at me, drawing me to sleep.

'For calling you here.'

'You had to.'

'But . . .' He looks away to steady himself.

He cannot explain, but I know already. Back in Marfa I was . . . lost somehow. The journey was necessary. The Zone has forged me. My companions were necessary. I could not have made the choice I made without them.

He peers into my eyes as if to check and check again that I am truly alive. 'Can you feel it?' he says at last.

Only then do I truly sense it. I have been immersed in it so long, reading its unfolding fronts, maintaining a perimeter, that to conceive its demise is hard. The Zone is no more. That spring-loaded presence is gone. The feeling that every mark and smell and sound is weighted with peril has just dissolved. The world is ordinary again. What takes me by surprise is my sudden grief at its passing. With the Zone goes its trackers, its mystery, its beguiling terror. For these past years we have been alive to it, or we have perished.

Pa consoles me. I see it in his eyes too, the loss. He clasps my hand and allows me the sweet devastation of the moment. I can at last be just a daughter.

My first steps are uncertain. Pa urges me to rest, to conserve my energy but I cannot lie like an invalid any more.

The sight of the fallen tether is mind-numbing. Always, our triumphs are bittersweet. Not every abductee has survived. Towns and cities have dropped like windfall fruit, fit only as seeds now. But for Kelly there is joy. I watch her from a distance tending to her mother and father. She runs over when she spots me, stops for a moment, then hugs me as hard as she dares.

'Hey, Megan,' she whispers through her tears. 'Humans: one. Aliens: zilch.'

Over her shoulder I see Luis. His smile is shy. In it I can tell that he does not care who or what I am now. We are together, three again.

At first I am too spent to move from the survivors' camp. But there are plenty of supplies commandeered from fallen towns. Away from the throng, we three build a bonfire. The only talk then is of practicalities – tending the flames, cooking the food. As we share a tin of pineapple chunks, I make a point of remembering the taste of the fruit – tart sunshine dribbling from my lips.

After the meal none of us speaks for a long time. Cisco

huddles close to the blaze for warmth. And we three watch as the sun sets at last. The spread of night is a salve to the soul. The stars that pass overhead are new ones. We point out the shapes they make – naming them.

Kelly says, 'Ice cream sundae.'

'What?'

'Can't you see it? Tall glass, vanilla scoops, cherry on top.'

'You can't name a constellation after a dessert.'

'And why the hell not? Look, it's even got a straw, with a bend in it.'

'Is just what you want right now to eat,' complains Luis. He searches my eyes as he says this. And when I meet his gaze, this time I don't look away.

Kelly fills the silence. 'Who says we gotta have the Great Bear or whatever? It's whoever sticks a label on it first I reckon.'

Our games quieten as the first of the crescents rises.

'Moons or planets?'

None of us know.

'Sure are pretty close, huh?'

There are three of them – pulling across the velvet black. One has rings. One is like a blue pearl. One is pitted and cratered like our long lost moon.

We usher in the dawn. The day strengthens into a punishing heat that we are not used to. The passage of the sun is like a miracle to me, and as I watch my shadow shrink and grow, I am impatient to break out of the camp, to see what world we live in now.

*

Our progress is slow by necessity. I can bear only a few hours in the saddle before I need to rest. But my strength returns with sleep and food. For days at a time we linger in the newly released land, hunting or fishing. The weather is fierce and changeable, as if goaded on by the spin of day and night. Life that has kept only a foothold in the old realms of Arizona and New Mexico burgeons again. Bats and birds return to their rhythms.

At Spider Rock we come with dread to the cottonwood and the cemetery. But all signs of battle have been erased. If Marshall fell in his last stand situation then someone else must have buried him. It gives me hope, because the Visitors would not have laid anyone to rest. So perhaps he lives still.

My father listens to our tales again and again. He revels in them, in the way Kelly plays each part, embellishing and exaggerating. They will, I'm sure, become folklore the way she steers them further from the truth. He is reticent about his own experiences. We will perhaps never learn how he navigated his way to confront the White Shell Woman of the Zone, how he sent Yiska into the wilderness with the keys to her destruction.

Once, alone, in that quiet cold before dawn, while the others are asleep, he tells me about my mother. He speaks of her with awe and warmth, about how they met and survived together in the Zone, how they worked to uncover its secrets.

'She was taken, Megan.' His voice is a whisper. 'I could not prevent it. The abduction was . . . slow. Though she fought it, she could not win. But she resisted long enough to give life to you. The birth was difficult. She kissed you and named you. And then she died in my arms.'

He gazes at the grey east light. 'I thought to keep you clear of the Zone, to protect you from it. I thought if you could stay on the border with your aunt, you'd be safe. But . . . the Zone was part of you. And over time, I suspected you even had the strength to fight it.'

'Pa, I . . . I nearly gave in.'

'Hush now.'

I think about my choice then. How I nearly embraced the Zone. What would I be now? A dark myth. My blood absorbed into the tether. A tyranny unfolding through the human race.

He takes my hand, but he does not look at me. Instead he waits for the sun.

There is an ease about my pa – the way he laughs or out-quips Kelly. Nothing left to prove, I suppose. And yet at times on that long journey back towards civilisation, I catch him staring at the new configurations in the night sky, and his face is fixed in concern. He won't discuss it, but I know the threat remains. We will have to pick through the pieces of Visitor technology. We will have to re-arm.

A quiet unspoken dread seeps into me as we approach the Deadline border. I mourn the Zone – its wildness. How long before the skies are parcelled up by flight paths? How long before we hear the sound of helicopter blades? I think that Marfa holds nothing for me, though I am hungry for news of the sheriff who saved my life.

At White Sands, though, the shadow that hangs over our future is banished, for now at least. The land rivers have run dry. And tilting at a rakish angle on a sand bank stands Marshall's house. His mule looks up from the trough on the pier. I throw off my hat in the race to reach his doorway. He stands there smiling, waiting for us on the porch, his arm in a sling, Nugget draped over his shoulder.

There is a new sign swinging in the wind. It says 'The Kimberlite Saloon.'

And we are his first customers.

ACKNOWLEDGEMENTS

Many thanks to my agent Veronique Baxter
who believed in this book from day one.
Also Barry Cunningham, my fantastic editors
Imogen Cooper and Christine O'Brien, and everyone at
Chicken House who worked to help bring my
western of the future to fruition.

Finally, I could not have reached "The End" without the
love, patience and insight of my wife Rebecca who
endured early drafts and supplied me with tea and wine
where necessary.

ALSO BY PHILIP WEBB

ISBN 978-1-906427-62-7 • £6.99

READ ON FOR CHAPTER 1 . . .

DEFINITELY NOT SCAV MATERIAL

SO I FIGURE IT'S JUST ANOTHER DAY RIPPING DOWN LONDON FOR US SCAVS, BUT I'M DEAD WRONG COS THIS IS THE SHIFT EVERYTHING GOES BALLISTIC.

First up, our crusher goes kaput, and that's a proper hassle cos we've got to de-clog the filters, which is *the* worst job, and we don't get a bean for it cos we ain't doing real scavving. And guess who's buried in the intakes up to their elbows in concrete powder with a glorified bog brush? Yep, when you're fifteen and a girl, you get all the plum jobs like that cos there ain't no one else on the team can fit in the damn intakes. Well, there's Wilbur, my kid brother, but he ain't in the frame. He'd probably just crawl up here and go to sleep. Bright as a pin, but anything scav-related goes right over his bonce. Anyhow, I'm trying not to think what would happen if the crusher was to crank up again right now, when the old man pipes up from outside.

'Where's Wilbur?'

And you know what? That don't even deserve an answer cos how the hell am I supposed to know?

But then he crams his head into the intakes and even through all the gunk on my goggles I can see he's looking jittery.

'There's been no sign of him since the crusher went down,' he hisses. 'Did you see him?'

I make a show of scanning the tiny space round my head. 'Dad, I ain't seen nothing but the end of my nose for the last hour. He's probably parked on his chuffer somewhere reading a comic.'

'I checked on all the floors. He's not there.'

I don't say nothing then, cos Wilbur's got previous on this. First chink of downtime and he's off nosing about on his tod instead of staying put like he's been told a million times before. And that's bad news on this side of the river.

Outside I can hear the gangmaster barking at everyone to get a lick on, even though there ain't nothing to do till I get these filters clear. He's narked cos every minute the crusher's out of action, he's losing, too. It means we'll be working double speed to play catch-up. And if we're shorthanded there'll be hell to pay.

Dad drags me out by the ankles just as the gangmaster disappears behind the crusher's tracks. 'I'll finish up here. You go and rustle him up. I can make out like you're still inside. And, Cass, don't hang around. I can't stall them for ever.'

'But —'

'Don't argue with me, Cass. Just do it.'

I suppose it makes sense but I don't like it cos we can't afford for the gangmaster to get wind of this. He's always on the look out for an excuse to ditch us from the crew cos we're slower than the others after Dad bust his leg in an accident and it set bad. So we could really do without my useless brother going missing . . .

I sneak into the gaff we've been scavving since the shift started.

'Wil-bur!' I call out — sing-song with a touch of the evil I'll do to him when I find him. I'm still hoping he's just holed up in a cupboard reading from his extensive collection of cartoon cobblers . . .

But it's kind of creepy quiet, like you know there ain't no one there.

And then it hits me where he's gone.

I grab up my gear — ropes, backpack, helmet — cos I'll stick out like a sore thumb wandering off-site without it.

By now everyone's crowded round the busted crusher – guards, boffins, scavs – so it's easy slipping out the far end of Little Sanctuary back across the wasteland towards the river.

Wilbur, what a right royal pain in the bejesus. He's been on about it for weeks, though I ain't paid it one ounce of attention. Cos it was just him blathering on. But I remember he was gutted when we wasn't detailed to be on the Parliament crews.

Luck loves me in one way cos it's the third morning of smog on the trot, a real snot-gobbler as they say, green and sopping from the dust and the fumes. Which means full mask and goggles is the order of the day, so no one clocks that I ain't meant to be there. 'Specially as demolition's at full pelt. This is the face of the scav-zone north of the river and there's got to be a thousand crews working the streets from Millbank to Embankment. But if you ask Wilbur (and I ain't asking), they're all wasting their time.

I hurry down Bridge Street, ducking between the pillars of the old shop fronts, blending in with other crews as they queue up to offload into the crusher chutes. If a gangmaster spots me I'll be in it up to my neck, but everyone's so pooped and bent double with their bins I don't get a second glance.

Man, Wilbur's got some explaining to do. Right after

I spifflicate him. See, he's got some notion he knows where the artefact really is.

Which is nuts.

Cos ever since the end of the Quark Wars, our lords and masters, the Vlads, been forcing scavs to tear down London to find it. A hundred years we been on the case! The Empire of New Russia, the conquerors of the world, with all their fancy machines, can't figure out where it is. But Wilbur thinks he's gone and figured it out just by reading some comics!

Course, the destination keeps shifting. A few months back it was in Churchill's bunker, down on King Charles Street. He was ready to bet his life on it. Till we heard that got picked clean without so much as a murmur.

Now he thinks it's in Big Ben.

It's quiet when I get there, what with the crushers out of earshot. I'm all knackered from the running so I spend a minute getting my breath back, just staring up at the lone tower. And I get a funny feeling about the place, the way it looms above me in the lime smog, caught in the river searchlights, looking spooky and proper lovely. Shame it's gonna be brick-dust inside a couple of months. I rip off my mask and goggles cos they're steaming up big-time. The rest of the Houses of

Parliament is just a honeycomb – scavved out to the bare bones and surrounded by mud canyons and mounds of slag. There's just a couple of teams at the far end ripping down the masonry. In a few days, they'll be ready to prep the tower. That's how it goes. Like starving ants we swarm into every nook of every building, one by one, from your garage to your palace.

Big Ben is gonna have its day.

But not today.

There's some old Portakabins and scaffolding round the base of the tower, and one of the first-floor windows has been busted in, which is probably Wilbur, so I climb up the scaffold and go in the same way past bits of glass. It's dark inside cos all the windows are coated with smog dust.

'Wilbur, you berk!' I yell.

Nothing.

'Wilbur, stop messing about!'

Silence. Just my boots scuffing around in the grit.

'The old man's gonna go mental if he finds out, so you better get down here pronto.'

My voice goes echoing up into the tower. I pull the torch out my pack and switch it on. There's a gloomy hall up ahead, pretty much empty apart from a few benches, and the start of a spiral stairway. Great.

Doesn't take much to figure out he's gone to the top, to the clock. Probably a hundred metres, and then some.

I tighten the straps on my pack and start up the stairway. For the first couple of floors there's landings with mouldy carpet going into the wreckage of the Houses of Parliament.

'Wilbur, you waste of space, I'm gonna burn every one of them damn comics when we get back, swear to God.' But I don't yell this, cos I'm done with yelling. And I don't mean it neither cos Wilbur's head's in the clouds, that's all. He don't mean no harm.

But then my heart just about jumps through my gob.

Someone's standing in the shadows right in front of me.

I stumble back against railings and my pack nearly tips me over the stairwell. I swing up my torch.

It ain't Wilbur staring back at me.

And that freaks me out even more. Cos why would anyone else be here?

It's a boy. Tall and wiry and wild-looking. His eyes blaze at me. And that's weird. He don't squint or shield his face – he just seems to soak up the torchlight. I hold the beam there, like it might hold him at bay. Cos I ain't sure what to make of him. Them eyes – green and clear and unblinking. Like a cat giving you daggers. And he don't look like any boy I ever seen around London. Definitely not scav material. He's got this crazy hair with clumps chopped out – done in a hurry. By the village idiot. With a blindfold on. And he's so clean you can see the black of his hair and even his eyelashes. I'd have to have a month of baths to look that shiny. His lips are pink and his hands . . . His hands are practically *royal* next to my scabby mitts. You never seen such beautiful hands, like on a statue. Still, the strangest thing is his threads, like military get-up but flimsy, more like a kid's idea of a uniform. About as useful for scavving in as a pair of pyjamas.

'Who the hell are you?' I go.

He don't answer. Maybe he don't speak English. Maybe he's a Vlad or a boffin. Except what's he doing here on his tod, creeping about in the shadows? And suddenly I remember about Wilbur and my hackles go up. Cos scavs have got all kinds of tales about survivor-mutants that creep about in the Underground tunnels, snatching kids and that. Or wanderers from the Northern Wilds. And I always figured them stories was cobblers but look at me now, trying to stop the torch from shaking. Except, the more I look at him, the more I calm down. Cos he's just too flippin' clean to be a baby-eating Feral.

'You seen my brother? Kid, so high, bit gormless.' I stop myself, realising this description is a tad pointless. 'Look, you seen *anyone* around here?'

He steps back, looking like he might make a run for it.

'Hey, slow down. I ain't gonna hurt you. You just scared the crap out of me, OK?'

He keeps his distance and steals a glance over the stairwell. Then he's straight back to me with his wary eyes, shivering a bit now in his bonkers outfit.

'It's just me. There ain't no one else . . . Look, do . . . you . . . speak . . . Ing . . . ger . . . lish?'

'I understand you,' he goes. He's got the queerest accent – *clean* you might say, like he's picked English up from a book. 'There's a boy. I saw him pass. He went higher, up there. I was going to call to him but I didn't want to scare him away . . .'

He trails off, probably cos he's twigged how dodgy that sounds. I'm thinking, *Yeah, but you didn't mind giving me the fright of the century, did you?* I turn to go, cos this is about the weirdest conversation I've had in yonks and it ain't helping me track down Wilbur.

'What are you all looking for?' he blurts out. It's like the words don't come natural to him, like he ain't done no speaking for a long time.

'What?'

'All you people. What are you searching for?'

I'm thinking, *Are you kidding? Surely everyone knows about the lost artefact . . .* But I ain't got time to answer him cos from way up above us in the tower comes the smashing of glass and a muffled cry. Wilbur!

I whirl away from the boy and charge up the stairs, three at a time, my pack slamming up and down with each stride. After a few flights I snatch a glance back and I see his shiny face staring up at me, then he starts following.

I bound up till it's two-at-a-time, then one-at-a-time, tripping, scrambling, then practically crawling on all fours. By the time I reach the top my blood's pumping so hard I'm seeing stars.

There's a bell. The biggest bloody bell I've seen ever, green with age, and if it was to sound off now I reckon it'd kill me stone dead.

'Wilbur?' My voice wheezes out like the last gasp of a mouse.

There's this passageway past all the cogs and innards of the clock, and it leads out onto the back of the clock face. And I can see grey daylight through it, the black numerals and the hands, and a hole near the spindle at the centre. But no Wilbur. I throw off my pack.

The boy stumbles into the space behind me, gasping and retching.

'Give me a leg up,' I go.

'What?'

'Jesus, do you speak English or don't you? Give me a bunk up!'

I show him how to link his fingers into a step, and he hoists me up the wall opposite the clock face where these old pipes and light fittings are. Somehow I scramble up the pipes onto the spindle, then inch to the hole in the glass. I see shreds of green smog, glints of the Thames, the last stumps of Westminster Bridge, far below.

My stomach goes to water. Wilbur's gone. Dear God, no. He's at the bottom now, and I've got to go down and find his body, what's left of it. And I've got to tell Dad . . .

And then I hear a whimpering cry. 'Cass?'

I practically slip over the edge with shock. Then, slowly, I lean out as far as I dare.

And right at the end of the minute hand is Wilbur, clinging on with everything he's got.